Transfixed in awe and wonderment, Allie scrutinized baby Jake

He was so small, so precious, so beautiful. And he'd practically been dropped into her lap by a good fairy.

Allie frowned. No, she was definitely romanticizing that part. And arrogant English aristocrat, Liam McAllister, had brought the babe to Allie's door and into her life.

But what had Liam meant when he said he wanted to be involved in "any and all decisions made about the baby"? Since he'd saved the infant's life, perhaps he had some continued concern for little Jake's welfare.

But the baby was in good hands now. The right hands. *Her* hands.

And that was exactly where he was going to stay— even if she did owe Lord Roderick big time....

Dear Reader,

What better way to celebrate June, a month of courtship and romance, than with four new spectacular books from Harlequin American Romance?

First, the always wonderful Mindy Neff inaugurates Harlequin American Romance's new three-book continuity series, BRIDES OF THE DESERT ROSE, which is a follow-up to the bestselling TEXAS SHEIKHS series. *In the Enemy's Embrace* is a sexy rivals-become-lovers story you won't want to miss.

When a handsome aristocrat finds an abandoned newborn, he turns to a beautiful doctor to save the child's life. Will the adorable infant bond their hearts together and make them the perfect family? Find out in *A Baby for Lord Roderick* by Emily Dalton. Next, in *To Love an Older Man* by Debbi Rawlins, a dashing attorney vows to deny his attraction to the pregnant woman in need of his help. With love and affection, can the expectant beauty change the older man's mind? Sharon Swan launches her delightful continuing series WELCOME TO HARMONY with *Home-Grown Husband*, which features a single-mom gardener who looks to her mysterious and sexy new neighbor to spice up her life with some much-needed excitement and romance.

This month, and every month, come home to Harlequin American Romance—and enjoy!

Best,

Melissa Jeglinski
Associate Senior Editor
Harlequin American Romance

A BABY FOR LORD RODERICK
Emily Dalton

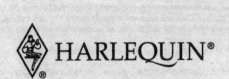

TORONTO • NEW YORK • LONDON
AMSTERDAM • PARIS • SYDNEY • HAMBURG
STOCKHOLM • ATHENS • TOKYO • MILAN • MADRID
PRAGUE • WARSAW • BUDAPEST • AUCKLAND

To Aimee, Lisa's second little miracle.
Your smile lights up the room!
With love, from your Auntie Danice

ISBN 0-373-16926-4

A BABY FOR LORD RODERICK

Copyright © 2002 by Danice Jo Allen.

Printed in U.S.A.

ABOUT THE AUTHOR

Emily Dalton lives in the beautiful foothills of Bountiful, Utah, with her husband of twenty-one years, two teenage sons and a very spoiled American Eskimo dog named Juno. She has written several Regency and historical novels, and now thoroughly enjoys writing contemporary romances for Harlequin American Romance. She loves old movies, Jane Austen and traveling by train. Her biggest weaknesses are chocolate truffles and crafts boutiques.

Books by Emily Dalton

HARLEQUIN AMERICAN ROMANCE
586—MAKE ROOM FOR DADDY
650—HEAVEN CAN WAIT
666—ELISE & THE HOTSHOT LAWYER
685—WAKE ME WITH A KISS
706—MARLEY AND HER SCROOGE
738—DREAM BABY
783—INSTANT DADDY
823—A PRECIOUS INHERITANCE
926—A BABY FOR LORD RODERICK

Don't miss any of our special offers. Write to us at the following address for information on our newest releases.

Harlequin Reader Service
U.S.: 3010 Walden Ave., P.O. Box 1325, Buffalo, NY 14269
Canadian: P.O. Box 609, Fort Erie, Ont. L2A 5X3

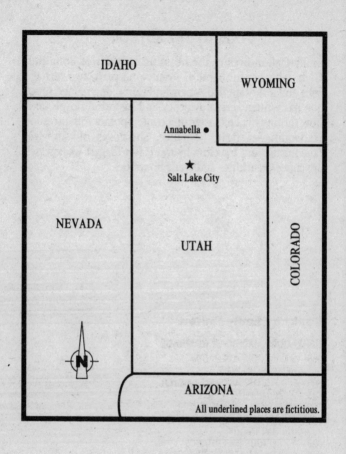

IDAHO

WYOMING

Annabella •

★
Salt Lake City

NEVADA

UTAH

COLORADO

N

ARIZONA

All underlined places are fictitious.

Chapter One

"I have to go, Daddy."

Liam turned his head briefly from the road and looked down at his small daughter in the seat beside him. In the wan light from the dashboard he saw she'd managed to curl herself into a comfortable ball despite the restraining seat belt. "I thought you were asleep."

Bea stretched a frail-looking arm in front of her, the heel of her hand jutting out like a crossing guard halting traffic, and yawned. "I was. But now I'm awake and I've got to *go.*"

Liam peered out the windows at densely wooded countryside, broken up now and then by open stretches he assumed were the meadows and alpine lakes he remembered from his last and only visit twenty years ago to this northeastern corner of Utah. It was nearly midnight, black as pitch outside, and raining. His visibility was limited, but he was sure they weren't passing petrol stations. The last one he'd seen of those was a neglected, two-pump enterprise in a bump-in-the-road berg nearly half an hour's drive behind them.

"We're almost there, Bea. Do you think you can wait till we get to Gran's house to go to the loo?"

Bea unfolded herself till her thin legs hung over the edge of the seat, pushed a tangle of brown curls out of her eyes, then started to squirm. "No, Daddy, I can't wait. I've got to go *now*."

Liam supposed he could pull over, fetch the umbrella he'd thrown in the boot of the rented car along with their luggage, and shield Bea from the rain while she squatted by the side of the road. But she'd just gotten over a cold and he wasn't too keen on the possibility of her getting chilled. She'd lost more weight in the last month and she seemed to catch every bug going around. Besides, she'd be embarrassed. She was only five, but she was as self-conscious as a teenager.

Suddenly they crested a rise in the road and he saw lights ahead. Relieved, he announced, "This is your lucky day, Beatrice Mary McAllister. That's got to be Annabella ahead. Just hold on a little longer, okay?"

Liam would be as happy as Bea to finally reach their destination. He'd traveled enough in the United States to be able to adjust quickly to driving on the right side of the road, but he'd driven nonstop from Salt Lake City and was jet-lagged and exhausted. They'd left the main highway, Route 150, quite some time ago and had been traveling along a dark, lonely road as jigsawed as a puzzle piece. And with Bea asleep, he'd had nothing and no one to keep him company but the rhythmic swish and muted thump of the windshield wipers, the resonating vibration of the tires on the wet road, and a country-music station that faded in and out depending on minor fluctuations in altitude.

It wasn't that he was afraid of falling asleep at the wheel. Nodding on the road had never been a problem.

But he'd been doing too much thinking. Since the tragedy that tore apart his world a year ago, he had avoided the quiet situations that left one tempted to replay the best and worst moments of one's life. But he was forced to agree with Gran that this trip, and the quiet that went with it, was something he could no longer avoid.

He slowed as outlying houses and buildings cropped up alongside the road. They all looked battened down for the night. "Let's just hope there's a petrol station or a restaurant open, because it might take a bit too long to locate Gran's house. She lives on the edge of town, about a quarter mile up one of these mountains, you know."

Bea sat up and peered over the dashboard. "Is there a McDonald's here?"

"I doubt it, sweetheart. This is the back of beyond."

"The back of *what?*"

Liam chuckled. "That's just another name for places like Annabella, Bea…towns too small and remote to attract a global hamburger chain."

"But even Bridekirk's got a McDonald's."

She was right. Even their tiny village back home in England had a McDonald's, built right across the street from the Nag's Head Inn, a pub nearly two hundred years old. While he'd been none too pleased when the colorful facade of a McDonald's had been wedged between far more venerable styles of architecture on the cobbled streets of Bridekirk, he'd give anything to see those golden arches now. The main street of Annabella looked as drenched and deserted as the last two towns they'd passed through.

"There, Daddy! I think I see a petrol station."

Liam followed the direction of Bea's pointed finger. It was a station, all right, but it was closed. "Maybe the loo's outside in the back. Cross your fingers it's open, or else we're going to have to find you a tree to pee behind. At least there's plenty of those."

Bea nodded and, instead of crossing her fingers, she crossed her legs.

Liam pulled off the road and behind the station where a yellow light flickered forlornly in the rain, revealing a small rubbish bin resting against the wall between two white doors, their paint blistered from the sun. He ordered Bea to stay put for a minute and made a dash through the rain to check the door marked "women." It was locked—or jammed—and the knob was sticky. He grimaced and, without much hope, tried the men's door next. The knob turned.

Liam gingerly pushed open the door and flicked on the light. He was surprised to discover the facilities relatively clean. Since there was no urinal, there'd be one less thing he'd have to explain to his curious daughter; the condom machine was going to be difficult enough to put a name and a purpose to. He rolled out some paper towels, wetted them and cleaned the toilet seat for good measure, catching a glimpse of his reflection in the mirror as he straightened to wash his hands.

He noticed, but wasn't distressed by, the way the indirect lighting in the washroom accentuated the smudges under his eyes and made his dark hair seem dull and lifeless. He had a five-o'clock shadow, too, giving him a gaunt appearance. His looks had often been touted by the British tabloids as comparable to Daniel Day-Lewis "in one of his hunkier roles." With an indifferent smirk at the haggard reflection staring back at him, Liam decided that Daniel should definitely be offended by the comparison.

He went back to the car, got the umbrella out of the boot and popped it open, then went to the passenger side and lifted Bea out, carrying her like an American football under his arm. She weighed next to nothing. He set her down inside the washroom and shut the door, waiting outside while she did her business.

Liam gazed where the lights of the idling Jeep Cherokee shone into a stand of spruce and aspen trees. He took a deep breath of rain-washed mountain air. It was cold...colder and wetter than he'd thought Utah would be in September, although perhaps it would warm up some once the storm passed. He was glad he'd dressed Bea in a sweater and jeans, but was still anxious to get her back inside the heated car.

Large raindrops plopped steadily against the top of the umbrella, dripped off its rim and made mini-explosions on the black asphalt at his feet. The noise was loud, but not loud enough to drown out the static of misery that crackled in the back of his mind. He was used to keeping busy to avoid those dark thoughts....

What was that? He cocked his head. Had Bea called him? He turned and tapped on the door with a single knuckle. "You say something, Busy Bea?"

"No, Daddy. I'll be done in just a minute."

Liam turned away and resumed his pensive observation of the weather. Then he heard it again. A faint mewling sound, like a kitten. It was coming from the rubbish bin.

Liam took a tentative step toward the bin, its lid propped open several inches by a large sack of garbage that stuck up above the rest. He peered inside the receptacle, which smelled pungently of decayed food and motor oil, and saw nothing moving. He stepped away, convinced that if a kitten was somewhere inside, it was better off there than outside in the storm.

The noise came again, but this time it sounded less like the plaintive crying of a kitten and more... well... *human.* Liam got a fluttering feeling in his stomach and told himself he was just imagining things. Surely that wasn't whimpering he heard. Whimpering, like a baby fussing in its crib. It had to be an animal of some sort, an animal that only sounded human.

A shaft of light appeared on the asphalt. "Daddy, I'm done."

Liam turned to see Bea in the doorway of the washroom, her arms crossed, her hands gripping her knobby shoulders. Quickly he scooped her up and carried her to the car. "Wait here, sweetheart. I've got to check something out. I think there might be a kitten or some other small animal in the rubbish bin."

Her face tilted to his, her eyes shining and hopeful. "Can we keep it? It must need a home or it wouldn't be sleeping in a stinky old rubbish bin."

He made a wincing smile. "We'll see."

He closed the car door and returned to the rubbish

bin. He knew he was probably being stupid, but he couldn't rest now till he knew what was making that noise. He hoped he wouldn't be racing to hospital in a couple of minutes to get a rabies or a tetanus shot...or both.

He waited till he heard the cry again—so pitiful and weak it tugged at his heart—then carefully but rapidly began to remove the garbage in the area he thought the sound was coming from. He felt an urgency that belied the rational voice in his head that kept telling him he couldn't possibly be unearthing from a rubbish bin something...*someone*...human. But stranger things had happened and life just wasn't fair. Some people were willing to die to bring a child into the world, and some people threw children away.

Underneath a large paper cup that dripped the sticky remnants of a soda and a mustard-smeared wad of fast-food wrapping paper, Liam found the source of the noise. He was so stunned and horrified, he thought for a moment he was going to vomit. He gulped back the bile and breathed what amounted to a prayer and a curse. "Dear God."

It was a baby. Wrapped loosely in a small, faded patchwork quilt, it lay with its head at an awkward angle against a grease-soaked paper sack, its fists raised above its bare chest, trembling and pale with cold. Its dark hair was still slick from the birth canal and the stump of its umbilical cord was reddish-brown with blood.

Liam forced himself to set aside his horror, his revulsion toward whoever had tossed this baby in the garbage, and focused on saving its life. He threw down his umbrella, pulled off his sweater, then gently picked up the infant. It was a boy. A boy like the newborn son Liam had lost a year ago…along with Victoria, his wife.

Liam discarded the sticky quilt and quickly wrapped him in the sweater, still warm from his own body heat. Clutching the child to his chest, he hurried to the car and slid into the seat. The baby felt so cold against him, Liam was scared to death it was too late to save him.

"Daddy, show me the kitten! Can we keep it?"

"Bea, it's not a kitten. It's a baby. He's very cold and I've got to get help quickly or he might—" Liam caught himself before finishing the sentence. But Bea was no dummy. Since her mum's death, his daughter was all too aware that bad things happened to people. She stared, her bottom lip caught between her teeth, while Liam reached with a shaky hand to turn up the heater full-blast.

He laid the baby in his lap and quickly rewrapped him in the sweater, taking care to cover his head but not obstruct his breathing. The baby had stopped the pitiful crying that had alerted Liam to his presence in the first place, but the quiet was almost more disconcerting.

He was tempted to rub the baby's skin to warm him up, but had a vague recollection of having read that that was not a good thing to do in hypothermia cases. As well, he had no idea whether or not hypothermia was the only danger this newborn was facing. Had he been injured during the birth? Manhandled afterward?

Were his lungs functioning properly? The dire possibilities seemed endless.

Holding the baby in the crook of his left arm and tight against his chest, Liam punched the car into gear and circled the station, looking for a phone booth. When he didn't find one, he pulled up to the road. He tried not to feel desperate as he looked up and down the dark street, wondering which way to go.

"Are we going to hospital?"

Liam heard the fear in Bea's voice, the residual terror of hospitals since her mum's death. He tried to give her a reassuring smile, but his teeth stuck to his dry lips. "We're going to find a phone booth and call for help, Bea, or knock on a door if we have to," he managed. "Don't worry, honey, we'll get help."

Bea's bottom lip quivered and her eyes brimmed with tears. "Please don't let the baby die, Daddy."

ALLIE WOKE UP with a start, soaked in sweat, her heart hammering, her mouth dry. She'd fallen asleep on the sofa in front of the television while watching *Sabrina,* the original one with Audrey Hepburn and Humphrey Bogart, and now an infomercial was on. A man gleefully pulverizing fruit in a mixer touted the benefits of a diet comprised only of juices, while a buxom blonde in a body leotard posed nearby and smiled vacuously.

Allie glanced distractedly at the digital clock on the VCR. It was ten minutes past midnight. She swung her legs over the side of the couch, propped her elbows on her thighs and rested her head against her trembling hands.

What a dream. What a horrible dream.

And it was still so vivid....

*She was sitting on the porch in Grandma Lock-
wood's squeaky old rocker. She held a baby in her
arms and crooned to it the same nonsensical words
her grandmother had sung to Allie when she was an
infant.*

*"Hi-dumma, do-dumma, hi-dumma-diddle-dumma,
hi-dumma-diddle-dumma-day."*

*Allie smiled contentedly into the baby boy's pink
and peaceful face. Her heart swelled with mother's
love.*

*Suddenly the precious weight of the baby's body in
Allie's arms disappeared. She found herself holding
only the patchwork quilt her grandmother had made
for Allie's firstborn. Terrified, she stood up and began
searching for the baby.*

*She looked everywhere. In his crib by her bed. On
the couch. Under the couch. Under the couch cush-
ions.*

*With the fantastical illogic of dreams she found her-
self looking in spaces no normal-sized baby could fit.
In the sewing box. Under the TV guide. Down the
bathtub drain. And all the while her horror and desperation grew.*

Where had he gone? Where was her precious child?

It was such a relief to wake up and realize there was
no baby to lose.

No baby.

Allie shook her head, wry and resigned. This was
the first time one of her baby dreams had ended badly,
but maybe it was her subconscious mind trying to
wake her up to the reality of her situation.

It had been going on for months. Three, sometimes four nights a week, she'd dream of a baby. It was a different baby each time, a child as real and individual and detailed in her morning's memory as if she'd held it in her arms the night before.

At first the vivid dreams frightened Allie. She thought her sterile state was making her, quite literally, go crazy. But, over time, she started looking forward to them. They filled a need. They allowed her to hold, to bathe, to nurse, to rock and to sing to babies of every description. Sometimes they were blond and blue-eyed, sometimes dark-haired, dark-eyed, and dark-skinned. The only thing they all had in common was that they were *hers*. Hers to love and care for.

Ironically the dreams hadn't started when Allie found out her fallopian tubes were nothing more than stringy cords of scar tissue and she'd never be able to have a child of her own. They hadn't started when she found out her husband of half a dozen years had been sleeping with Rhonda Middleburger, the waitress at Bill and Nada's Diner, nor did they begin when she and Doug divorced nine months ago. They'd started just when she thought she'd come to grips with the realities of her life.

It had been New Year's Eve. In the first moments of the new year she'd made an important resolution. She was going to quit feeling sorry for herself. So what if all she'd ever dreamed of beyond obtaining her medical license was to be a mother, to fill her house with kids and noise and the type of wonderful family chaos she'd enjoyed in the home she'd grown up in? She, Althea, was destined for something different. No children, no noise, and, apparently, no husband, either. But that was okay. She'd have a wonderful, full life anyway.

"But first maybe I need to see a shrink about these dreams," Allie grumbled to herself as she reached for the remote to turn off the TV. "It was weird enough when they were *nice* dreams, but—"

Allie was startled by the sound of the doorbell ringing, then a fist hammering on the front door. She dropped the remote and hurried down the hall toward the front of the house, straightening her oversized, sleep-creased flannel shirt so that the buttons at least marched in a straight line between her breasts. She ran a hand through her short blond hair, but knew she must still look a mess. Whoever was on the other side of that door probably wouldn't care, though, or even notice how she looked. As a doctor in a small town she'd been summoned from bed many times to take care of an emergency, but most people called first and told her they were coming.

"Allie, you in there? Open up!"

It was Doug's voice. His tone wasn't cajoling or tender, so he must be knocking on her door in his official capacity as Sheriff instead of for the usual reason he bothered her in the middle of the night.

"I'm coming!" she called, flipping on the lights as she jogged through the living room, then made short work of the dead bolt lock that secured her front door. When she'd purchased the security item at Harv's Hardware, Harv had just looked at her, wondering, she supposed, what she thought she needed with a dead bolt in a town where no one bothered to lock their doors. She marvelled now at the irony of willingly opening her door to the man she'd meant to keep out by installing the dead bolt in the first place.

"Doug, what's wrong?" The words were spoken as she opened the door, before she was able to look past her ex-husband's tall, uniformed figure to an even taller man standing just behind him.

Now she was speechless. It had been years since she'd last seen Liam McAllister in person. *Twenty* years. He'd been thirteen years old and she'd been eleven. He'd spent a week that summer with his grandmother and Allie had spied on him for hours at a time from the tip-top branches of the big cottonwood tree on the edge of Mary McAllister's property.

Since then Allie had heard of Liam, read about him and seen his pictures as part of numerous media stories. The public's fascination with the former playboy aristocrat turned devoted husband seemed insatiable, and reporters had relentlessly stalked him through the sad and happy dramas of his life till he must have felt like screaming...or finding a secluded island to escape to.

But why on earth to Annabella? To see Mary, she supposed. But what was he doing on her front porch in the middle of the night instead of Mary's, and why did he have such a stricken expression in his eyes?

"Allie, we've got a sick child here. Maybe dying." Doug slipped past her frozen form and into the living room. Liam followed, along with a small, thin girl who clutched the back of his shirt. She appeared frightened and pale, but hardly at death's door.

Confused, Allie bent down and peered into the child's pinched face. "Don't you feel well, honey?"

"It's not Bea," Liam said shortly. "It's the baby."

Allie straightened up. She'd registered the name "Bea." She'd read that Liam had a five-year-old daughter named Beatrice, nicknamed Busy Bea, but she'd never seen a picture of her because Liam refused to allow her to be photographed. She'd read about and sympathized with his tragic losses a year ago, but since his premature son had died along with his wife that terrible day, Allie wasn't sure what baby Liam was talking about.

She gave a helpless little shrug. "What baby?"

Allie had been so shocked to see Liam, she hadn't noticed that he was clutching what looked like a balled-up sweater in his arms. Now he tipped his bundle toward her and turned back the sweater to reveal a baby, sallow and still, its umbilical stump raw from an obviously recent birth. Allie's breath caught in her throat, rattled there for a stunned, horrified moment, then gushed out with her next words.

"Bring him back here to my office."

Chapter Two

All business now, Allie jogged ahead of them to the back of the house where the three rooms that constituted her home office were located adjacent to the den, where she'd just been sleeping in front of the television and dreaming of a baby. The dream coinciding with a real baby's arrival at her office would seem weird...if she didn't dream about babies most of the time. She flipped on the bright overhead lights, making everyone wince and blink, then immediately moved to a large stainless steel sink and turned on the hot water tap.

"Whose baby is it?" she asked over her shoulder as she soaped up her hands and rinsed them in scalding water.

"We don't know," Liam answered. His brows drew together as he closely observed her movements. "I found him in a rubbish bin."

"The Dumpster behind Johnsons' Gas 'n Go," Doug clarified.

Allie's whole body revolted at the idea of someone putting a newborn baby in a Dumpster to die a cold, miserable death. She was again stunned into momentary silence and immobility. Liam's frown stirred her to action, though, and she quickly grabbed a wad of paper towels and dried her hands. "When?"

"Fifteen minutes ago," Liam said, then abruptly, "What's taking you so long? Shouldn't you be *doing* something?"

"I am doing something," Allie replied calmly, attributing his uncivil tone to worry and fear. "You don't want him to get an infection on top of everything else, do you? Put him on the table."

Allie noticed a muscle ticking in Liam's jaw as he laid the baby on the examining table. Then, without being told, he spread his hand on the baby's midsection to keep him from accidentally rolling off—unlikely with a newborn, but still you couldn't be too careful—leaving Allie free to rummage through her supply drawer.

She ripped open a sterile plastic bag containing an infant-sized oxygen mask, attached the tubing to the free-standing tank by the table, adjusted the flow and placed the mask over the baby's nose and mouth.

"Hold this over his face, while I adjust the strap."

Liam obeyed instantly, one hand holding the mask in place while the other hand remained securely on the baby's stomach.

Allie found it rather unnerving ordering Liam around, and she didn't suppose he was at all used to it. But she had learned to be as bossy as necessary when it came to saving lives, not holding back even when male egos were involved...or in this case, the ego of a viscount with the fancy-schmancy title of Lord Roderick, who also just happened to have been the romantic hero in some of her more vivid girlhood fantasies. She supposed it was all those hours in the tree, watching him, making up stories about him....

She grabbed the digital thermometer from the countertop and swiped the probe with an alcohol swab.

"Do you need me?" Doug demanded. "Because if you don't, I'd better get back to the Gas 'n Go. I've called Lamont and I'm meeting him there."

Allie looked up. "You called Lamont out tonight?" Lamont was the county's Crime Scene Investigator.

Doug nodded curtly. "Attempted murder is pretty serious stuff, Allie. Got to get the evidence while it's fresh."

Murder. Allie could hardly believe something like this was happening in Annabella. She nodded, then said, "Go to the hall closet and get the small quilt Grandma Lockwood made, please."

Doug immediately turned and headed for the door. She caught sight of Bea hovering just behind her father, trembling with either excitement or fear. "Get a blanket for Bea, too," she called after him.

Doug was a lot easier than Liam to order around, even if he only did what he was told when he wanted to, or really needed to, as now. Besides, he knew where everything was.

She turned back to the baby, pushed the sweater just far enough aside to expose his bottom, and inserted the probe. She could have used the ear thermometer and got an instant reading, but she'd found the rectal thermometer to be more accurate and it took only a few seconds longer.

Liam kept his hand on the child's chest and stomach, his fingers making tiny, caressing circles. With his free hand, he reached back and rubbed Bea's neck and shoulders, trying to calm her. Once upon a time Allie had watched those hands whittling sticks, building a birdhouse, digging in the dirt for nightcrawlers or for stones to skip on the pond by Mary's house. Liam's grown-up hands were elegantly shaped, the fingers long and tapered, the nails immaculately groomed.

But it was the way he was trying to comfort both children at once that made her smile up at him and say, "Don't worry. I think the baby's going to be fine. By the looks of him, he has only a mild case of hypothermia…thanks to you. You must have found him very soon after the birth. You did just the right thing bundling him up in the sweater and finding help. I'll know exactly what to do, too, as soon as I get this temperature reading."

Liam didn't return her smile. His green, matinee-idol eyes stared back at her for a moment, then his gaze shifted to the baby. Her overture rejected, Allie felt a little stab of hurt, of annoyance.

The thermometer beeped and she read the temperature with a sigh of relief. She was tempted to smile, but remembered the response to her first smile and didn't. "Just as I thought, his temperature is only slightly below normal. We can treat him here and save him the trauma of a trip to the hospital tonight, particularly since it's still raining like gangbusters. He'll be much safer, warmer and dryer here than en route to a facility seventy miles away."

Liam straightened up and pulled Bea against his side. "I called the operator from a pay phone. She told me to wait there for the sheriff. He showed up about two minutes later—which was quite a relief—then I followed him here. But I assumed he called for an ambulance. Wouldn't that be routine?"

Allie picked up her stethoscope and hooked it around her neck. "Not necessarily, but we'll ask Doug. On a night like this, we'd be lucky to get one. Our nearest ambulance center is located in Kamas, same as our nearest hospital. They both service an area that's sparsely populated but very large in terms of miles. And getting to some of the more remote areas can be tricky on the system of highways we've got in this part of the state. We've learned to take care of what we can on our own, or drive like the wind to get someone to Kamas if there's a life and death situation."

Liam gave a slight, disapproving shake of his head. "What if *this* had been a life and death situation? What if it still *is?*"

Allie was now convinced of something she'd suspected all along…that Liam didn't have a gnat's worth of faith in her abilities. Again she told herself that he'd just been traumatized and was probably not his usual charming self.

She took a deep breath and forced an understanding smile. "Trust me, Lord Roderick, the baby will be fine. I really do have the situation under control."

At his continued doubtful scowl and silence, she spoke up again, this time her words more clipped and pointed. "I may practice in a rural area, but I've still got all the skills necessary to be a doctor. There's no time to poll the townspeople for an opinion of my abilities, but I've got a pretty darn good reputation. If you've got doubts about my credentials, however, my framed diplomas and certification documents are displayed over my desk in the next room.''

If Liam was chagrined by her mild sarcasm and felt an urge to apologize, Allie didn't wait to find out. She fit the stethoscope to her ears and listened to the baby's heart and lungs. Although slightly tachy, his pulse was strong and had a regular sinus rhythm. His respirations were a little shallow, but the airways sounded clear as a bell. There was nothing unexpected, nothing she couldn't treat right there in the office.

Next she removed the oxygen mask—he was pinking up very nicely already—and checked the baby's pupils and reflexes. They were normal. Then she gently moved the baby's arms and legs, probing and testing for possible breaks or bruises. He seemed fine, but follow-up X rays at the hospital tomorrow would be a good idea.

During the entire examination, the baby didn't make a peep. He just lay there, listlessly staring. Allie figured he didn't have the energy to cry, but she'd soon fix that.

Doug came back in the meantime and confirmed her suspicions that he hadn't bothered to call an ambulance at all. He'd decided to wait for Allie's take on the situation. Despite everything else wrong with their relationship, at least Doug believed in her abilities as a doctor.

Now her ex-husband was standing at her elbow,

looking uncomfortable as he held out the small quilt. Allie understood his discomfort. Grandma Lockwood had made and given the quilt to Allie in anticipation of a great-grandchild, and had died still believing that she and Doug would someday have a baby of their own. Allie had always intended to give the quilt to someone who could actually use it, but despite lots of friends and relatives having babies, she just couldn't bring herself to part with such a precious gift. It would be like giving away a dream.

After Allie took the quilt, Doug handed a regular-size blanket to Liam. Liam had picked up Bea in his arms to cuddle and soothe her while Allie examined the baby, and now he quickly settled her in a chair by the door, tucking the blanket snugly around her from neck to toes.

Bea remained silent, but her worried look must have prompted Liam to say with a reassuring smile, "Don't worry, love. No need for the hospital. The doctor says the baby's going to be just fine." Then he stooped and kissed her on the top of her head.

Bea's pinched little face relaxed a bit. Now if only Bea's father actually believed what he was saying, Allie thought wryly.

"Anything else you need before I go?" Doug asked.

"I've got premixed bottles of formula in that bottom cabinet in the kitchen by the fridge. You know, where I've always kept the bottled water? Heat one for a minute or so under the tap. Room temperature would normally be fine, but this little guy could use something warm."

Doug hesitated, staring down at the baby with a worried look on his lean, tanned face. "Is he really going to be all right?"

Allie was glad he'd had the tact to whisper the question. "Yes," she assured him. "If he doesn't take the bottle, though, I'm going to do an IV. We need to get his blood sugar up and some fluids in him."

Doug, still rooted to the spot, dragged a hand through his thick blond hair, his expression part disbelief and part grim fury. "Hell, Allie...who could have done this?"

Allie shook her head. "I don't know. I thought I knew everyone who's pregnant around here and I can't imagine any one of them doing such a thing. Besides, if you're pregnant, then suddenly you're not, people are going to wonder what happened to the baby. It would have been a noticeable pregnancy, too, because this baby looks full term."

"Well, whoever it was deserves to be strung up...or thrown naked into the same Dumpster on a night like this. Hopefully there'll be plenty of evidence at the station that will help us find the mother."

"Well, get me the bottle, so you can go," Allie said. "I'd ask Lord Roderick, but he doesn't know how to get around the house like you do."

Doug flicked a surprised glance at Liam, obviously recognizing the famous name. The name was even more famous in Annabella than it was in other more sophisticated parts of the world—or perhaps it would be more correct to say "infamous." Liam's grandmother had a history with the town that had become local lore. Hazarding her first direct look at Liam since her reprimand, she saw, and thought she understood, his grimace. He hated being recognized.

"Doug...?" Allie prompted.

Doug left the room. Liam gave Bea another reassuring pat before walking back to stand next to Allie. "You should have let him go," he said. "I think I could have found the kitchen if I'd tried. England's another country, not another planet." After an infinitesimal pause, he added, "Or maybe, because of my title, you don't think I've ever been inside a kitchen?"

Allie looked up at him, surprised. "Believe me, I haven't given any thought to what rooms you may or may not frequent, Lord Roderick. Why are you being so touchy? I know you're stressed out over this. We *all* are. I didn't mean to insult you...even though you don't seem to mind insulting *me.*"

He looked equally surprised. "When did I insult you?"

"You didn't think I knew what I was doing and was worried that I was going to—" she lowered her voice "—let the baby *die.*"

"No. *No,*" he objected. "It's not that I thought you didn't know what you were doing. It's just that he's so small, and he was so cold and so—" He stopped abruptly and shook his head, his disapproving scowl replaced by a more appropriate look—in Allie's opinion—of sober concern. "Never mind. I'm sorry if I've been rude. But do you think a bottle is enough? Why not do an IV just to be sure?"

Softened by his apology, Allie altered her tone and answered patiently. "Despite what they show on all those hospital TV shows, starting an IV isn't always the first thing a doctor does when a patient is brought in for emergency treatment, Lord Roderick.'' She stooped to tuck the blanket around the baby and lift him gently into her arms. ''I think we can—''

Her sentence trailed off as she absorbed the shock of an immediate, almost overwhelming surge of feeling for the child as she settled him against her chest and smiled down into his small face. He had the usual newborn look, complete with squinty eyes and a slightly misshapen head topped with sticky black hair.

Allie thought the baby was beautiful…cone-shaped head, squinty eyes and all. The feel of him, the welcome weight of him in her arms, was just like one of her dreams.

''You were saying, Doctor?''

Allie realized that Liam was staring at her, and his disapproving scowl was back. Caught feeling foolish and vulnerable as she drooled over her dream-baby, she tried to sound as professional as possible.

''As I was saying, I think we can stabilize this child without drugs or invasive procedures. His hypothermia is mild and he checks out normally in all other respects. He just needs to be wrapped up, snuggled in someone's arms and given a warm bottle. If he's too sluggish to suck, we'll do an IV. Later, once his temperature's risen sufficiently, we can put him in a warm bath and get that blood and gunk off him.''

Unable to resist the urge any longer, she threw her professional image to the wind and bent to lingeringly kiss the baby's sticky forehead. ''Poor little thing smells like the dump on a warm day,'' she whispered.

Liam said nothing and Allie didn't dare look at him. Besides, she was perfectly content looking at the baby.

Doug was back with the bottle. "I tested it, but you'd better test it, too."

Allie agreed. Doug knew squat about babies and bottles. But to Allie's surprise, the temperature of the formula was just right.

"It's fine, Doug. Thanks."

"Then I'll be going." He was already striding toward the door. He pointed a finger at Liam. "I'll need to talk to you some more, so don't leave town, Lord...er...."

Liam winced. "If you don't mind, I'd rather you— *all* of you—weren't so formal. My name is Liam, and I have no intention of leaving town for at least a month. Oh, and look by the rubbish bin...er... *Dumpster*...for a patchwork quilt like that one." He motioned toward Allie and the baby. "He was wrapped in one very like it when I found him."

Doug nodded briskly and left, allowing Liam to turn his full attention back to Allie and the baby. She wished *his lordship* would leave, too. She'd give anything to be alone with the baby so she could feed him and enjoy him without feeling watched and self-conscious. Certainly this unsmiling peer-of-the-realm would find something wrong with the way she was holding the bottle or question the wholesomeness of the formula brand.

Sure enough, just as she raised the bottle to the baby's lips, Liam interrupted.

"Can *I* hold him and give him the bottle?"

"No, I need to monitor his response firsthand."

Liam looked skeptical but backed away. He leaned his hips against the counter, crossed his arms over his chest and fixed his intense gaze on Allie and the baby. He may have backed off, but he was still staring at her.

Fortunately Bea's imploring expression must have caught his attention. Looking contrite and concerned, Liam went to Bea, lifted her up and slipped into the chair, settling her comfortably in his lap.

Now both of them were staring at her.

"Shouldn't you call your grandmother?" Allie asked on a sudden inspiration. "I'm sure Mary's worried sick by now. There's a phone on my desk in the next room." She couldn't resist adding, "Oh, and while you're in there, please feel free to look over my medical credentials."

Liam gave her a baleful look, which she answered with a guileless smile. He left, carrying Bea in his arms.

Allie finally had the baby to herself.

Smiling down at him, she observed that his color was already much better. Normal, in fact. Now, if she could just get him to take the bottle. But his eyes were closed. He might have fallen into an exhausted sleep.

She touched the rubber nipple to the baby's lips, a tiny drop of warm formula seeping out to pool in the corner of his mouth and dribble down his chin. "Come on, sweetie," Allie coaxed. "I know you're tired. This has been a doozy of an opening act, but now's not the time for a siesta. Open up. I think you'll like this. It's going to make you feel much better."

The baby's eyes fluttered open. His mouth caught

the nipple and clamped onto it. *Thank God for the sucking instinct,* Allie thought.

The baby's forehead furrowed with surprise as he took a couple of involuntary swallows. His eyes widened, blinked twice, then drifted shut as he continued to suck. Allie gave a sigh of relief and smiled, her heart swelling with that wonderful "motherly" feeling she'd experienced before only in her dreams.

MARY ANSWERED halfway through the first ring.

"Hello?"

"Gran, it's me."

"I've been worried, Liam!"

"I know. I'm sorry. It took us longer to get into town than I expected, then Bea had to go to the loo and we stopped at a petrol station."

"At a petrol station? Nothing's open this late in Annabella. Where are you, Liam?"

"We're at Doctor Lockwood's."

"What's wrong? Is Bea sick?"

"No, Bea's fine. I'm fine, too."

"Then why—?"

"It's a long story, Gran. I'll tell you everything when I get to the house."

"How soon will you be here?"

"In just a few minutes." Liam hesitated, then asked, "How well do you know Allie Lockwood, Gran? Has she been in Annabella long?"

"Allie's family's been in Annabella since the dawn of time, just like mine. Our tribe moved away, but she and...a couple of her family stayed on."

"Okay, so she's a longtime resident, but is she a good doctor?"

"I've never needed her services, thank God, but everyone swears by her around here. If she's half as good as her grandfather was, though, I'd say she's an excellent doctor."

Mary's voice had gone suddenly wistful. That's when Liam remembered something he'd heard about Annabella. Something he'd been too distracted to remember sooner. *Lockwood.* Lockwood was the name of that man from Gran's past. The man she'd jilted to marry his grandfather. He'd never heard the whole story before and was suddenly consumed with curiosity, but now was not the time to drag out skeletons.

"Liam? Why do you want to know if Allie Lockwood's a good doctor? I thought you said you and Bea were fine?"

"We are."

"But—"

"Bea and I will be there in just a few minutes, Gran. I'll explain then."

"All right, then. See you soon. I'll have hot chocolate ready for you."

"Goodbye, Gran."

"Goodbye, love."

Liam hung up and looked down at Bea, curled up in the corner of a small sofa in Allie Lockwood's tiny cubicle of an office. She looked so tired, so frail, so anxious. As traumatic as the past hour had been for him, he imagined it had been even worse for her. And he'd been so preoccupied with making sure the baby was okay, he'd neglected her a little. He forced his lips into a smile.

"Gran's got hot chocolate waiting."

Bea nodded. "Good. But what about the baby, Daddy?"

"I told you he's going to be all right, Bea."

"I know, but…but are we just going to leave the baby here? Who's going to take care of him?"

"Doctor Lockwood, for now. As for later, I don't know, Bea. Probably—"

Bea's brows drew together and her large brown eyes darkened. "Because I've been thinking, Daddy," she said in a tone that struck Liam as being heartbreakingly serious and grown-up for such a small child. "Why can't we take care of him? He needs a home, doesn't he?"

"It's not that simple, Bea."

"I think God sent him. We lost our baby, so God sent us another baby to take his place."

Sure, if life was fair, if there really was justice in the world, Liam thought to himself, the infant he'd found tonight might be able to help fill the void that had been left by the deaths of his wife and child. And the baby *would* be needing a home.… But Liam wasn't even an American citizen. And with the circumstances of the baby's birth and the crime committed still unknown, he'd be crazy to get involved. He'd done his part by fishing the baby out of that rubbish bin and now they must part ways.

"It doesn't work that way, Bea," he finally answered. "But we'll talk about it again tomorrow, if you want. Right now Gran's waiting for us. Let's go say goodbye to Doctor Lockwood."

Bea struggled up from the couch and looked so pale and weary, Liam picked her up in his arms, keeping the blanket snugly wrapped around her.

Bea giggled. "*I'm* not a baby, Daddy. You don't have to carry me."

"But just this once, you don't mind, do you?"

She put her arms around his neck and tucked her head under his jaw. "No, I don't mind."

Liam walked to the door of the examination room and looked inside. Allie stood with her back to them, gently swaying back and forth. One elbow was in the air, as if she was holding a bottle. Good. The baby must be taking the formula.

"Doctor Lockwood?"

Allie turned around and the radiance on her face startled Liam.

"Oh, you're leaving?" she said. She looked and sounded pleasantly dazed, and not at all displeased that they were about to depart. It struck him then that her attachment to the baby was unnaturally quick and unprofessional.

In fact, if looks could kill, he'd have been dead the minute he suggested giving the baby the bottle instead of her. But all Liam had wanted was to hold him just once more, now that he was safe. To hold him without that awful feeling that he might die in his arms at any moment. Was that so much to ask?

As he stared at Allie Lockwood and the baby he'd fished out of a rubbish bin, Liam suddenly realized that it wasn't going to be possible to simply part ways with this child. And he wasn't going to wait for God to fix things and make them fair, either. It was impulsive and possibly stupid, but Liam determined at that moment that *he* would play God for once and try to bring about a little justice of his own.

"I'm leaving, but I'll be back," he told Allie. "I care about that baby and I want to be involved in any and all decisions made about him."

Before Allie could answer he turned and left the room, but her radiant look had been replaced by one of suspicious dismay. He knew he'd come across as arrogant and had undoubtedly overstepped his bounds…especially considering he had no rights whatsoever in the matter. In fact, he knew his whole manner from the moment they'd arrived with the baby had been abrupt and rude. He supposed his painful concern for the baby's welfare was the reason he'd behaved so badly, and he shouldn't have taken it out on Allie Lockwood.

But, he admitted, there was another reason he'd reacted to the doctor the way he had. The thing was, Allie Lockwood seemed to be finding it just as impossible as he was to be emotionally objective about this baby. She was so proprietary. *Too* proprietary. Did she want the baby, too?

Liam set his jaw. Too bad if she did. Besides, what was stopping her and her Sheriff boyfriend from making babies of their own? They had to be an "item." What other explanation was there for Sheriff Renshaw's familiarity with Allie's house?

DOUG HAD NEVER SEEN such a bloody mess in his life. It was all he could do to keep his dinner down. Sure, Annabella wasn't known for its violent crime and he'd only been on hand for a couple of domestic disturbances that involved shootings, but not even Homer Bledsoe's gushing neck wound had prepared Doug for the women's bathroom at Johnsons' Gas 'n Go.

Whoever had given birth to that baby had lost a lot of blood doing it. Which made him wonder if it wouldn't be a good idea to check the hospital at Kamas for recent admissions. He'd better check the morgue, too.

"I smell like hell." Lamont Johnson, the county's one and only full-time Crime Scene Technician, was standing in the Dumpster in waist-high garbage. "Kelly's not going to let me in the house tonight."

"Why should tonight be any different, Lamont?" Doug stripped off the latex gloves he'd been wearing and carefully put them in a plastic bag, tied it off and stuffed it back inside the pouch on his belt.

Lamont snorted. "You're one to talk. Allie's still lockin' *you* out, I hear."

"You shouldn't listen to gossip. Besides, my situation with Allie is different. We're not married anymore."

"Just wished you were, eh?" Lamont straightened up, pressing his knuckles into the small of his back. "I'm done here. There's more than enough evidence in the blood samples I collected to match DNA to a likely suspect."

Doug grabbed the tight muscles at the back of his neck and grimaced up at the dark sky. It had finally stopped raining, but the clouds still blocked any hint of stars and moon.

"There's the rub. We haven't got any suspects. And besides the blood, all we've got is that ratty old quilt."

Lamont struggled out of the Dumpster. "Think Captain Hightower will send you some help?" he asked on a grunt as his feet hit the asphalt.

"Maybe if I ask for it. But I'm not going to ask. This is my town and I know it better than any of those jokers Hightower might send me from the main office. I know the people and I know how to talk...and not talk...
to them. I'll have better luck with this investigation if I do it on my own and in my own way. Besides, if news of this got beyond Annabella that that royal pretty boy, McAllister, found the baby, the national media might grab hold of it and the town could be overrun with paparazzi. It's best if we try to keep this local, and Hightower agrees."

Lamont nodded and hiked up his drooping pants. "Well, that makes sense. But you're taking on a lot, Doug. If you don't have a clue who the perpetrator is, you're goin' to be doing a helluva lot of overtime."

Doug shook his head and gave a ragged sigh. "Lamont, when I think about how hard Allie and I tried to have a baby, then someone just throws one away like that... The whole damned thing just makes me want to puke."

Lamont snapped off his gloves and gave Doug a keen look. "I guess you really want to solve this case?"

Doug nodded grimly. "Yeah, Lamont, I guess I sure as hell do."

Chapter Three

Allie made a crib for the baby out of a Xerox box that her copy paper had come in and put it beside her bed on a wide-bottom chair. As she'd brushed her teeth and washed her face in the bathroom just two feet away, she'd hurried out at the slightest movement or sound the baby made, staring down at him with anxious concern.

As soon as she'd convinced herself that he was just fine, her worried scrutiny changed to a transfixed sort of awe and wonderment. She'd stand there, staring, for minutes at a time, toothpaste dripping off her chin, soap burning her eyes because she'd run out of the bathroom mid-rinse. But she couldn't seem to help herself. He was so small, so precious, so *beautiful*. And he'd practically been dropped in her lap by a good fairy.

Allie frowned. No, she was definitely romanticizing that part. A very disturbed mother had abandoned her baby in a Dumpster and an arrogant aristocrat—not a good fairy—had brought him to Allie's door and into her life.

As Allie climbed into bed, she thought about Liam

McAllister and their rather contentious exchanges. Gradually she concluded that she'd been too hard on him. Overwhelmed by her own feelings for the baby and astonished by the rightness of his suddenly appearing in her life, she'd completely forgotten that Liam had good reasons for having some rather overwhelming feelings of his own.

He'd lost a child just a year ago. A baby boy, like the one he'd found. There was a sort of bittersweet irony in the fact that he'd saved this one, but hadn't been able to save his own little boy. An irony that probably had not been lost on Liam. No wonder he had been watching and questioning and criticizing everything she'd done. She needed to give him some slack, be more understanding.

But what had he meant when he said he wanted to be involved in "any and all decisions made about the baby"? Since he'd saved the baby's life, it probably was quite natural that he'd have some continued concern for the baby's welfare, but she certainly didn't want him becoming a nuisance. The baby was in good hands now. The right hands. *Her* hands. And that was exactly where he was going to stay.

There was no denying, though, that she owed Liam McAllister big-time. If it hadn't been for him, the baby would have died in that Dumpster. Allie shivered at the thought and slipped out from under the covers to scoot the chair closer to her bed. If she sat upright with the pillows plumped up behind her, she could stare down at the baby without getting out of bed.

Allie banished all thoughts of Liam McAllister and smiled contentedly. She didn't need baby dreams now.

She had the real thing. In that moment she decided on following through with the impulse that had seized her the first moment she held him in her arms. She was going to adopt him.

LIAM STOOD on the redwood deck and enjoyed the sight of the sun filtering through the pine trees on the eastern border of Mary's property, his hands curved around the warmth of the stoneware mug filled with hot coffee. Except for the brief foray into the kitchen to fetch his dose of morning caffeine, he'd been standing there since just before sunrise. Everything was fresh and bright after the storm, and today there wasn't a cloud in the sky.

Despite his jet lag and the emotionally exhausting ordeal he'd been through, he'd only managed to sleep about three hours.

"Liam?"

Liam hadn't heard the glass doors sliding open. He turned and saw his grandmother standing half in, half out. She was a petite woman and seemed tinier than ever in the oversize flannel robe she'd wrapped herself in. He recognized the red plaid robe as his grandfather's. "Hi, Gran. Sleep well?"

"As well as any old lady sleeps. How about you? No, don't tell me. I can see you didn't sleep a bit." She stood on the deck with him for a minute, looking out at the same vista he had been enjoying for the past couple of hours. The sun glinted off her silver hair and made it look like spun sugar.

Finally she took a deep breath of the crisp mountain air and said, "Come in and have some breakfast."

Liam obeyed. He wasn't hungry, but he had to keep his strength up. Besides, Mary got talkative over toast and tea and he had some questions.

As Liam crossed the large great room toward the adjoining kitchen, he remembered how his grandfather, the Earl of Chiltington, used to call this huge edifice "Mary's little cabin in Utah." True, it was made of logs, but it wasn't little and it could hardly be described as a cabin. With four bedrooms, five bathrooms, a great room, a modern kitchen, a library and wraparound decks on three levels, it was more like a charmingly rustic mansion.

Mary had protested when her husband had the plans drawn up for building it. She'd only wanted to update the stone cottage her parents had retired to on the same site and left to her in their wills. She was an only child, therefore the only recipient of their small amount of worldly goods.

As usual, Liam's grandfather had won the day. He said the property was big enough to build a new house on it and still keep the cottage as a sort of guest retreat. He needed more room if he was going to be spending a bit of every summer in Utah. Besides he just might bring a few jolly friends over with him from England from time to time, and the children and grandchildren must always have a place to stay.

The irony was that Mary had spent two weeks each summer in Utah every one of the twenty years after the "cabin" was completed, while her husband, who had promoted the grander design, had only managed to make the long trip over from England once. He'd stayed a week, then hurried home to his pub, his horses and his hounds. He didn't mind leaving Mary behind, because he knew she would soon follow.

Cecil McAllister, Lord Chiltington, was an English country gent through and through, and Utah just didn't cut it for him. But he understood Mary's love for the country of her birth and they parted amicably for those two weeks each summer, then came together again, ecstatic to see each other and full of family plans for the rest of the year.

As far as the rest of the McAllister clan, Liam was the only family member to spend time with Mary in Utah, and then only once, that first year.

Two years ago, Liam's grandfather passed away, and last year and this year, too, Mary's stay in Utah started in June and extended through the autumn months. She would return to England and her children, grandchildren and great-grandchildren in time for Christmas, but not before. Liam suspected that she was being drawn more and more to her roots and wondered if she'd finally end up spending most of each year in Utah.

Liam smelled bacon frying and saw Ribchester and Mrs. Preedy busy in the kitchen. They were elderly servants who had been in Gran's employ since the 1950s. Gran was seventy-eight and Liam guessed Ribchester and Mrs. Preedy—who were married, but still went by their "professional" names—were in their midseventies, as well. Despite their protests, Mary worked about the house almost as much as they did, so they were more like companions. But Mary let them do the cooking because that had never been one of her talents.

"Over easy as usual, my lord?" Ribchester inquired, waving his spatula and looking odd in the tailored jacket he insisted on wearing with a green checked apron, appliquéd with a large moose head, over it.

"That would be perfect, Ribchester," Liam answered. "But only one this morning, thank you."

Ribchester acquiesced without comment, but he and Mrs. Preedy exchanged frowns. They'd fussed over him since he was a child and had never got over the habit. He supposed he should have ordered two eggs just to make them happy.

"Bea's still asleep," Mary said, as she eased down into a chair by the table. "I looked in on her before coming downstairs. She's exhausted from the trip."

"And everything else that happened last night."

Mary shook her head and gratefully clasped the handle of the mug of tea Mrs. Preedy set in front of her. "Thank you, Mrs. Preedy." After a sip, she continued, "I could hardly believe it when you told me. I've heard of people leaving unwanted babies in rubbish bins and loos and such, but I just never thought something like that could happen in Annabella. And that you, Liam, after all you've been through, would be the one to have to deal with something so horrible."

"I'm glad it happened," he said.

"Well, of course you are. I didn't mean—"

He put his hand over hers. "I know what you meant."

They were silent for a couple of minutes, sipping their coffee and tea, thinking. Then Mary said, "Bea's so thin, Liam. Just since June I can see a difference.

And it's not just that she's getting taller and stretching out."

Liam nodded solemnly. "Yes, I know. I'm hoping this trip will help her."

"So am I. And I'm hoping it will help *you*, too. You both needed to get away. Neither of you were bouncing back from Victoria's death as you should. It's been a year."

"Is there a timetable, Gran?" Liam asked with a sigh.

She patted his knee. "No, I suppose everyone has their own timetable when it comes to grief. But when one is getting too thin for one's own good..."

"She doesn't talk about her mother anymore. She just..." He shrugged, lost for words.

"She's internalizing it. Perhaps she *needs* to talk."

"I took her to a therapist, but that didn't seem to help. In fact I took her to *two* therapists."

Mary pursed her lips. "I'm sure therapists do a great deal of good for many people. But in Bea's case, I can't help but think a good country doctor with practical knowledge and a friendly demeanor that encouraged confidences would probably be much better at drawing out the child."

"Are you hinting that Bea ought to be seen by *Annabella's* country doctor?"

Mary looked abashed, as if she'd said more than she meant to. "Well, I—"

"Which one? Allie or her grandfather?"

"Allie's the doctor now, not Jacob," Mary answered evasively.

"But I thought you didn't know anything about her?

How do you know she'd be someone Bea could open up to?"

Flustered, Mary gave a helpless little shrug. "I've *heard* she's an excellent doctor. Fortunately I've never needed her services. You know I don't mingle with the townspeople, so what I know is what I hear from Ribchester and Mrs. Preedy after trips to town. They gather a bit of gossip as they gather the groceries."

Suddenly she brightened. "Is this your roundabout way of asking me if I know anything about Allie Lockwood's *personal* life?"

"I'm not asking you about Allie Lockwood at all, Gran, and you know it," Liam said gently. "When you talked of a country doctor, you were thinking of Allie's grandfather, Jacob Lockwood, weren't you?"

Looking startled, like a child caught with her hand in the cookie jar, Mary set her mug down on the table with a thump. The tea spilled over the brim and onto the pine tabletop. She mopped up the tea with a green checked napkin, her eyes fixed to her task. "Perhaps I was," she finally admitted.

"Tell me about him, Gran."

"Well, he's a good doctor, too, although he *is* retired, you know."

"At the present, I'm not interested in his abilities as a doctor."

She finally braved a look at him. "Then what *are* you interested in, Liam?"

"I know there was something between you and him, bits of which I've heard a little of over the years, but now I want to know the whole story from start to finish."

"It's really ancient history."

"It's why you don't go into town, isn't it? And why no one visits you when you stay here? That doesn't sound like ancient history to me."

Liam had had all night to think about Allie Lockwood, the baby, and his grandmother's history with Allie's grandfather. He wasn't sure why he'd never been curious enough about it to inquire before, but he supposed he had been so involved with his own life, and Mary had been so happy with his grandfather, he hadn't felt the need. Now he wanted every bit of information available about that family and how it was connected to his, no matter how trivial the connection might turn out to be.

Mary sighed and tapped her fingers gently against the side of her cup. "It's a very simple and short story, Liam. I was raised in Annabella, as you know. My father was the pharmacist at Woolworths and Mother stayed at home...as most women did then. Jacob Lockwood teased and tortured me all through grammar school, but when we both turned thirteen, things changed."

A shy smile curved his grandmother's mouth, making her seem suddenly so much younger. "He was my sweetheart all through high school. We were going to move to Salt Lake City, so Jacob could go to the University of Utah, where he had a scholarship. He'd take premed, then go on to medical school. But first we'd get married."

"Then the war came and changed all that," Liam said.

Mary nodded sadly. "Yes. I wanted to marry him

before he joined up, but he refused. He didn't think it was the right thing to do. Times were so uncertain.''

She seemed to get lost in thought for a minute, then continued. ''Jacob was in the Navy and stationed in the South Pacific. I got frustrated waiting for him, waiting for his letters. Sometimes months would go by. I wanted to do something, not just sit about the house waiting and wondering.'' She smiled ruefully. ''We were a patriotic bunch back then, Liam.''

''It's a good thing you were,'' Liam replied quietly.

''I became a WAC and trained as a nurse. I was immediately sent over to England. I met your grandfather in the hospital in Dover. He'd had a head injury and didn't even know who he was. I fell in love with him, Liam. I couldn't help it. I didn't know who he was, or anything about him, but I knew we were meant to be together. I know that sounds sickly sweet, but it's true.''

Liam had no trouble believing her. He'd felt the same way about Victoria. ''Go on.''

''We were married by the chaplain at the base. I hadn't heard from Jacob for over a year. I wanted to tell him about Cecil before the wedding, but I had no address. I wasn't even sure he was still alive. Two months after our wedding, Cecil's father found him. I was nearly bowled over when I heard Cecil was going to be an earl someday and owned country estates in Cumbria! I thought he was just some bloke from London.''

''Not with that high-brow accent of his, Gran,'' Liam teased her.

''Well, I didn't know about accents then, Liam. It

took a few months, but your grandfather gradually re-gained his memory.

"I was afraid he'd regret marrying me, when he could have had just about any girl in England, but he didn't. His parents—your great-grandparents—were a little floored at first, but they learned to accept me, too. I've been very happy with your grandfather, Liam. But my heart ached for Jacob...."

"What happened to Jacob?"

"He was injured in the war, too. Sent home in '44 with injuries to his back and both legs. For awhile no one thought he would walk again. I hear he still limps."

"And when he found out about you and Grandfather?"

"By the time Jacob heard about it, the townspeople had decided that I'd dumped Jacob—a war hero with a Purple Heart—to marry a rich English lord. My parents said he took it hard, drank like a fish for awhile, but he was always a stubborn one. He swore off liquor, then worked hard till he could walk again, then he went on to medical school and came back to Anna-bella to be the best GP they'd had in these parts...or so I've been told. He married Allie's grandmother, Al-thea Rutherford, and they had one child, a boy they named James. James married another Annabella 'belle' named Lisa, and they had four children. Two boys and two girls. I think you played with the boys that summer you briefly visited, Liam...."

"Oh?"

"Yes, but the boys moved away, as did their parents, but Allie and Kayla, the two sisters, still live in Annabella.''

"Is this Dr. Lockwood still alive and living in Annabella?''

"Oh yes. He's retired, as I told you, but he didn't move away. I don't expect Jacob would ever leave Annabella.''

"How about his wife?''

"Althea died several years ago.''

"Ah, so he's a widower.''

Mary's eyes narrowed. "So?''

"You've come here every year for twenty years, but you never go to town. You just go through it when you're coming from, or going to, the airport. You send Ribchester and Mrs. Preedy to do the shopping. It might have been an easy thing to manage when you used to come for only two weeks at a time, but now that Grandfather's gone and you spend months here, I imagine it's pretty difficult to keep away from the only bit of civilization there is around here. What keeps you away, Gran? And why doesn't anyone come to see you? Surely the townspeople don't still hold a grudge?''

"I don't know whether they do or not,'' Mary replied with an unconvincing show of unconcern. "They probably don't. I'm sure they've had better things to do over the past half-century than harbor resentment against *me*.'' She paused, then added wistfully, "Even for Jacob's sake...''

Presently she said, in a firmer tone, "Besides, the town has grown and changed. There's still people I know, but their grandchildren probably haven't even heard of Mary Hayes McAllister.''

Remembering Sheriff Doug Renshaw's reaction from the day before, Liam wasn't so sure that was true. If Doug had heard of him, he'd heard of his grandmother, too.

''So the bottom line here, Gran, is that you're not that worried about facing the townspeople. It's Dr. Lockwood you're worried about running into in the produce department of the grocery store. Right?''

Mary nodded grudgingly. ''I admit it, Liam. It's Jacob I'm avoiding. I don't know why, but I still can't face him.''

''People don't plan on falling out of love with someone and in love with someone else,'' Liam reasoned. ''It just happens. You weren't married to him. He wouldn't hold a grudge against you after all these years if he's the great guy you say he is…or *was*.''

Mary shook her head. ''I don't know, Liam. I just don't know.''

Liam was then served his breakfast and he noticed that Mrs. Preedy had made up for the lack of two eggs by supplying him with twice as much bacon and several slices of fried tomato. Liam preferred a bowl of oatmeal or fruit for breakfast, but Mrs. Preedy still believed in a hearty English breakfast and he didn't mind indulging on those rare mornings he spent with his grandmother. He smiled up at Mrs. Preedy, who was still hovering anxiously, and gamely picked up his fork.

''You really should be asking about Allie Lockwood, you know," Mary presently informed him. "I hear she's a looker."

Sure, Allie Lockwood was a "looker," Liam had to admit that, now that he actually thought about it. Last night he'd been too shocked and busy to think about it, but he *had* somehow managed to notice that she appeared to be very curvy under that shapeless flannel shirt she was wearing, and had lips like Catherine Zeta-Jones...that slight, natural upturn at the corners of her mouth even when she wasn't smiling. *Kissable* lips.

Fortunately Sheriff Renshaw had dibs on those kissable lips, and they were, therefore, off-limits. Not that Liam had given the idea of kissing them a second thought.

"Ribchester and Mrs. Preedy aren't keeping you up on the latest, Gran," Liam informed her. This announcement, of course, caught the couple's attention and they turned and listened from their posts in the kitchen. "Sheriff Renshaw knows his way around that little house of hers like the back of his hand. They obviously have something going."

Ribchester's chest swelled and he smirked with the superior delight of someone who knows something someone else doesn't.

"I beg to differ, my lord," he said, striving to keep a humble tone. "Sheriff Renshaw knows his way around Dr. Lockwood's house because they *had* something going."

"They were married," Mrs. Preedy finished with a decided nod, "but got divorced nearly a year ago."

Ribchester and Mrs. Preedy stood motionless in the

kitchen and Mary smiled over her teacup at him, all
three watching for his reaction, but Liam hardly knew
how to react. All night he had thought of Allie Lockwood as being with Doug Renshaw. He'd thought of
it in the context of the town's doctor and sheriff marrying, and how that would prejudice the courts in their
favor if Allie wanted to adopt the baby. But now he
realized that thinking Allie was involved with someone else had, in a way, mercifully prevented him from
acknowledging an attraction to her.

Liam said nothing and began to industriously cut up
his fried tomatoes. Ribchester and Mrs. Preedy were
forced to resume their tasks in the kitchen, and Gran
held her tongue while he dealt with this new revelation
of his attraction to a woman for the first time since
Victoria's death.

So what? he finally concluded to himself. No matter
how physically attractive he found Allie Lockwood—
and it was only a physical attraction, since he hardly
knew her and what he knew he wasn't sure he liked—
he was not about to have a fling with a woman he
might possibly be facing in court in a battle over an
abandoned baby they'd both fallen in love with.

His initial impulse was to squelch any idea his
grandmother had about him linking up with Allie
Lockwood romantically. Mary meant well. She
thought he'd shied away from dating long enough. But
his grandmother was a hopeless romantic and didn't
realize how ridiculous the idea was even without
knowing his intentions regarding the baby. In more
than the literal sense, there was an ocean between Allie's world and his.

Then it occurred to Liam that details about Allie's private life might come in handy if there *was* a court battle.

He wasn't going to let Mary in on his plans just yet—he wasn't going to confide in anyone at all—so he'd have to be a bit dishonest about his interest in Allie Lockwood.

"All right, Gran. What else do you know about Allie Lockwood?"

Mary's face lit up, making Liam feel guilty as hell.

"I'm so glad you're curious! That's a very good sign. Trouble is, as I told you already, I don't really know very much." She turned to face the kitchen. "Have I told them all we know, Ribchester?"

Ribchester leaned on the counter with his hands. "Well, mum, there is a bit more."

"Oh good! What do you know?"

"A sad thing, really. Sheriff Renshaw cheated on her, is what I've heard, mum. That's what broke up the marriage."

"Yes," piped up Mrs. Preedy, standing over a sink full of soapy pans. "But he was a bit rowdy and irresponsible all along, I heard. I think his fling with the waitress was the straw that broke the camel's back, so t'speak."

"How dreadful!" Mary clucked.

"But he's not given up on her," Ribchester added. "People say the sheriff's still in love with her."

"Oh, well, I hope she's smart enough not to let that rascal back into her life," Mary declared.

"He's a handsome devil," Mrs. Preedy said with a dire look and waving a sudsy knife. "Many a woman's head's been turned by a pair of bonny blue eyes.''

Mary's glance slid to Liam…as he knew it would. ''But what good luck for Allie that the bonniest pair of *green* eyes I've ever seen just arrived in Annabella.''

Liam was about to gently end a conversation he'd let, perhaps, go to far. He was spared the trouble by the ringing of the doorbell.

When Ribchester returned from answering the door, Sheriff Renshaw of the ''bonny blue eyes'' followed him into the room. And the sheriff looked none too happy.

As soon as the sun rose, Allie was up and warming a bottle for the baby. She fed him, burped him, changed him into some baby clothes she'd tucked away in a dresser in the spare room (which had been destined for a nursery at one time), then rocked him till he fell contentedly to sleep again. She took a lightning-fast shower, with the baby's box just outside the door, and dressed quickly. By seven o'clock she was standing outside her sister, Kayla's, neat brick bungalow, ringing the doorbell.

She had to ring three times before Kayla finally answered the door. She was dressed in her usual outfit of a baggy sweatshirt and pants, and her mass of curly, strawberry-blond hair was disheveled and hanging in her eyes. She was pale and bleary-eyed.

''Kayla, you look like something the cat dragged in!'' she blurted out, then added more sympathetically, ''Up all night with Travis again? Or are you sick?''

Kayla pushed her hair aside and gave a weak smile. "Not sick. Your first guess was right. Travis was up till three this morning. He just wouldn't go to sleep. And for your information, sis, most people don't look so hot when they've been dragged out of bed after only four hours of sleep. What are you doing here? And what have you got in that box?"

Allie slipped past her into the house. "I still think you should bring him into the office again so we can discuss the possibility of medication for Travis."

"You know I don't believe in that stuff. Besides, he's only like this in spells. He's not always hyper."

Allie sat down on the sofa, placing the box beside her. "Maybe it's his diet. Like I said, bring him in again and we'll talk."

Kayla rubbed her eyes. "I will...when I get a chance."

"Kayla, you know you don't have to pay."

"But I want to."

"Don't be ridiculous—"

The baby moved in the box, engaging Kayla's attention again. "I hope you haven't got a kitten or a dog in that box, Allie. If you do, don't you dare show it to Travis. I don't need a pet right now. Can't afford one. I'm barely making ends meet as it is. Brad's support check bounced again."

Allie scowled. "That creep! Men who don't pay child support should be hung by their thumbs, or some other part of their—"

"I know what you think, sis, and I appreciate the sentiment, believe me. But that doesn't help the situation. Carol Hobbs was going to have me baby-sit Mi-

chael, but her mother offered to baby-sit for free and
that took care of that.''

"I think I can help you out, Kayla.'' Allie felt herself smiling uncontrollably.

Kayla sighed and dropped into a chair across from
the sofa. Allie felt guilty being so happy when Kayla
was so obviously tired and depressed. She had her
hands full with three-year-old Travis, but she was a
wonderful mother and a great cook and housekeeper.
Brad had never deserved her, and he'd done everything he could to undermine Kayla's self-confidence,
which had never been that great to begin with.

In their three-year marriage, Allie had watched her
sister go from plump to pregnant to very overweight.
Although she kept her house immaculate, as the
pounds came on she seemed to lose interest in her own
appearance. Then Brad left and Kayla started living in
sweatshirts and -pants, never went out, and devoted
herself completely to Travis. She did baby-sitting
when it came her way, which wasn't that often in such
a small town. She also did crafts that she sold in the
little boutique on Main Street, making a bit of money
to supplement the child-support payments.

Allie helped her financially whenever Kayla allowed her to, but she didn't like taking money from
her big sister. They had a close relationship, but Allie
occasionally felt an undercurrent of resentment ema-
nating from Kayla. She knew Kayla thought her older
sister had done much better for herself, which Allie
found hard to believe. Sure she made a decent living,
but her marriage had gone down the tubes, just like

Kayla's, and at least Kayla had little Travis to show for it.

Finally Kayla broke the silence. "I know you're good for another handout, Allie, but I can't keep taking your money."

"No, I'm not offering money. I'm offering you a job."

Kayla smiled ruefully. "Doing what? You know I can't work outside the home with Travis to take care of, and I can't afford a baby-sitter. Besides, I'm no nurse."

"But you're a great mother and a great baby-sitter." Allie gestured toward the box. "I would like you to baby-sit the contents of this box."

Now Kayla looked completely puzzled. "What? Baby-sit a puppy?" Her eyes widened. "Don't tell me you have a lab monkey in there?"

"Why don't you come see what I've got in here?" Allie suggested with another happy grin.

Kayla stood up and walked across the short distance that separated them. She looked into the box and just stood there for a couple of minutes, her puzzled expression changing to surprise, then quickly back to puzzlement.

She turned to Allie. "There's a baby in there."

Allie giggled. "I know. Isn't he beautiful?"

Kayla turned back to the box and stared for another minute or two. "Yeah, I guess he is. But who does he belong to? Are you starting a baby-sitting service now, Allie, as part of your practice?"

"No. He's mine, Kayla."

Kayla quickly turned back, her look incredulous,

her tone almost scornful. "What do you mean he's yours? When did you give birth? Besides, you're—"

Her happiness deflating a little, Allie said quietly, "I know I'm infertile, Kayla. You don't have to remind me."

"I'm sorry. I—"

"Never mind."

"Okay, so how—?"

"He was abandoned last night at the Dumpster behind Johnsons' Gas 'n Go. A man going through town found him and—"

"What man?"

"Well, this part will be hard to believe," Allie admitted. "It was Liam McAllister." Kayla looked at her blankly. "You know, *the* Liam McAllister?"

Kayla returned to her chair and sat back down with a thump. "Oh my God. Tell me everything, Allie."

Ten minutes later, Kayla was in possession of all the facts. At least everything Allie knew.

"And you're planning to adopt him…just like that?" Kayla snapped her fingers. She looked stunned. She'd looked stunned since the beginning of the story and still looked like someone had hit her upside the head.

Allie was starting to feel defensive. "Well, why not? I knew what I wanted to do—what I *had* to do— the minute I held him. Besides, he was *abandoned,* Kayla. His parents obviously don't want him."

"But there are rules, Allie. There's a process you have to go through." She stood up again and walked over to the box, staring down at the baby. "And, for

God's sake, you have to quit carrying him around in a box! He needs a car-seat and a crib, and—''

"Of course! I know all that. But I haven't exactly had time to take care of all those details. My first thought was to bring him to you to baby-sit while I see an office full of patients this morning. On my lunch break I'll call my friend, Ann Hansen, at Social Services in Kamas. I'll arrange to be his temporary foster parent. I know they'll agree to it because foster parents are at a premium, and since I'm a doctor and he had kind of a difficult birth—''

"What do you mean?" Kayla quickly asked.

"Well, Kayla, he was left in a Dumpster on a freezing cold night," Allie answered in an exasperated tone. "I'd say that's a pretty harsh way to come into the world."

"I know," Kayla agreed impatiently. "I mean, he looks perfectly normal to me. But is he hurt or sick?" She reached down and pushed the blanket away from his face to better examine him. Allie stood up and stared with her. The baby was sleeping peacefully and looked pink and healthy and extremely content.

Allie smiled and bent to stroke his soft dark hair. "I don't think he's either, which is a bit of a miracle. But I'm still planning on taking him to the Kamas hospital tonight for X rays. As I told you, he was only mildly hypothermic when Liam found him, and then he managed to warm him up some before he brought him to the office."

"Then after you've done the foster child thing, you plan to adopt him? Really *adopt* him, Allie?"

Allie laughed. "Why do you look so surprised,

Kayla? You know I've always wanted children. Being a single mom shouldn't throw a wrench in things, either, not in this day and age. Besides, I have a lot of influence around here.''

Kayla nodded and murmured, ''Yes. Yes, you do. But what if the mother shows up? Or…or the father? Won't there be an effort made by the police to find out who abandoned him? Despite what either of them might have done, they'll have rights.''

''They *shouldn't* have any rights,'' Allie said sternly.

''I just don't want you to be hurt, Allie. You could get your hopes up, then—''

''I'm not worried about anyone coming to claim him. I just knew somehow when I first held him that he belonged to me…you know? You've experienced that because you felt it with Travis.''

Again Kayla nodded and shrugged, her brow unfurrowing for the first time in the last fifteen minutes. ''Yes, I *do* know how it feels. And if that's how you felt when you held this baby, Allie, I guess you're right to go ahead with this.''

Allie smiled and stood up, impulsively hugging her sister. ''So you'll watch him for me?''

Kayla returned her hug and smiled back. ''Sure, I will. I can use the money. And you can use the help, that's for sure. I don't think you've got a clue how all-consuming it is to be a mother, though. Especially a single mother.''

''Well, I guess I'm about to find out.'' Allie turned and headed for the door. ''I'll be right back. I've got formula and diapers in the car.'' Suddenly she turned.

''I think we should quit calling him 'the baby,' don't you? I want to name him Jacob, after Gramps. Jake, for short. What do you think?''

Kayla shook her head wonderingly. ''You're pretty sure you know how this will turn out, don't you? You don't have the slightest doubt that you're going to get exactly what you want?''

Allie's smile was broader than ever. ''Who's going to stop me?''

Chapter Four

It was nine o'clock that night by the time Allie got home from the hospital in Kamas. Little Jake's X rays had been perfectly normal and she drove back to Annabella with a grateful heart and a head full of plans.

She pulled into the driveway and pressed the garage door opener, then parked inside the garage. She got out and opened the back door of her sedan and peered into the baby carrier/car-seat she'd bought during her lunch break that day. Jake had slept the whole way home, but now the cessation of movement and the light had stirred him from his nap. His tiny eyes blinked and his mouth opened, then instinctively shaped into a round "O." He was hungry.

"Just a minute, little one," Allie whispered, as she undid the seat belt that held the baby carrier firmly in place. "You'll have a warm bottle in just a—"

"Dr. Lockwood?"

Allie reared up and hit her head against the door frame, then whirled around. "Who's there?"

A long shadow loomed and then Liam McAllister stepped into view. "Don't be alarmed, Doctor. It's just me."

Allie's hammering heart slowed to something resembling a normal rate. She rubbed her head and said accusingly, "You scared the heck out of me, creeping up like that out of nowhere."

"I was parked out front when you drove up." He motioned toward his Jeep Cherokee, parked in plain view in front of the house. "I thought you saw me."

Allie wasn't about to admit she was so lost in happy daydreams that she hadn't noticed the Jeep, or anyone sitting in it. "I thought you were someone visiting the neighbors. Besides, most people come to the door and ring the bell. They don't ambush you in the garage. *Criminals* do that."

"I was under the impression that Annabella harbored very few criminals," Liam said dryly. "I had no idea you'd be so easily startled."

"If my nerves are a little frayed, it's because I didn't sleep much last night," Allie defended herself, still gingerly prodding her scalp. *"Ouch."*

Liam stepped closer. The weather had warmed up from the day before and he wasn't wearing a coat, only a crew-neck charcoal-gray sweater, dark slacks and...a look of genuine concern. That look of concern surprised and touched her, and she reminded herself that last night she'd decided to go a little easier on him, but here they were already off to another bad start.

"You hit it that hard, did you? I'm sorry."

His apology softened her attitude even more and she resolved to try very hard to be nice. "I guess it's not your fault *entirely.*"

He smiled. She had to admit he had a wonderful

smile…when he used it. "Why don't we go in and I'll have a look at it?"

This drew a wry chuckle from Allie. "Hey, who's the doctor here?"

"How are you going to look at the top of your own head?"

"With a mirror."

He raised a brow, looking very skeptical and very British at the same time. "I'd like to see you try. You'd have to be a contortionist."

Her chin came up. "Maybe I am."

He chuckled. "You're a very independent woman, aren't you?"

"Gramps says I'm stubborn."

"I don't know you well enough to just blurt out the truth like that."

"If you don't know me well enough to be truthful," she argued, "what makes you think you know me well enough to invite yourself into my house?" Uh-oh. There she went again, not being nice. What was it about him that pressed all her buttons? Maybe he was just too good-looking, and that activated all her defense mechanisms. After all, Doug's considerable good looks had probably seduced her into staying with him longer than she should have.

Liam raised his hands in mock defeat. "I only wanted to help."

Jake began to cry. It wasn't a loud, insistent cry, just an "I'm hungry, don't forget about me" kind of cry. It instantly drew Liam's attention and he moved closer and stared down into Jake's baby carrier. Even in the dim garage, Allie could see how Liam's eyes lit up.

"You were waiting for me," Allie said. "You didn't know I'd be hitting my head on the car door. You didn't come here to *help*."

"No, you're absolutely right," he agreed, without taking his eyes from Jake. "I came to see how the baby was doing." Now he looked up. "I'm sure you understand my interest."

He spoke so calmly, so reasonably, Allie chided herself for getting paranoid. Of course he'd want to check up on the child whose life he'd saved the night before. Once again she reminded herself of the tragedies he'd endured just a year ago, and she resolved to be more understanding and accommodating.

"Of course you can come in," she said with a sigh. "You can even help me cart some of this stuff inside."

But instead of grabbing the bags from her mad dash to the grocery store at noon—among her many other errands—he bent down and picked up Jake's baby carrier and the diaper bag. Then he stood back and waited for her to lead the way. Exasperated and trying not to show it, she carried the two admittedly lighter grocery bags herself, unlocked the door leading into her kitchen, and stepped aside while he walked through with the baby.

Without waiting for directions or instructions, he went straight into the living room and flicked on some lights.

Allie pressed the button to close the garage door and put her grocery bags on the kitchen table. Jake was still emitting a thin wail of hunger, so she hurriedly found a bottle of formula and set it under hot tap water. As soon as she felt it was warm enough, she grabbed it, dried it with a paper towel and hurried into the living room.

When she got there, Liam had Jake out of the baby carrier and cradled in his arms. He looked up from the couch when he heard Allie enter the room, saw the bottle, and held out his hand for it.

Allie didn't know why, but the sight of Liam holding Jake set off an alarm in her brain that went well beyond the protective instincts of a mother.

LIAM KNEW he'd alarmed Allie by taking the baby out of the baby carrier, and now practically demanding to be allowed to feed him. He decided that, in this case, at this moment, truth was the best policy. "I wanted to feed him last night…remember? I wanted to see what it felt like to hold him without worrying that he might die on me." He paused, then admitted with a smile, "It feels wonderful, by the way."

He could see her relenting. She might be stubborn, but she apparently had a kind heart.

"All right," she said. "I guess you earned the right to have a turn at feeding him." She handed him the bottle, then sat down next to him and watched avidly. She was sitting so close, he could smell her perfume. Something woodsy and spicy. Not like Victoria's powdery, floral scent, but nice and…well…different.

The baby sucked vigorously. Obviously his rocky start was only a minor setback for this little fighter. Liam's heart swelled with feeling.

Allie reached over and gently stroked the baby's hair. "Jake likes to eat, and the formula doesn't bother him. A mother's breast milk is best, of course, but I can't supply that at the moment."

Jake! She'd named him already! And her use of the term "mother," relative to her and the baby, rankled Liam, but he didn't dare show it.

She really does mean to keep this baby.

If Allie knew his own intentions, she'd cut him off from the baby immediately. Wouldn't let Liam near him. This just confirmed Liam's decision to keep all his plans to himself till he and the top-notch California lawyer he'd hired today had built an unbeatable case.

He tore his eyes away from the baby and rested them on Allie. She was wearing a very soft-looking pink chenille sweater, and slim black slacks. She was dressed very femininely, compared to the night before…although he'd have to say she looked equally fetching in flannel. But that was not something he should be thinking about.

"I gather you just returned from the hospital in Kamas?"

"Um-hm."

"So, how did the X rays look?"

"They were perfect. Every little bone was perfect." She glowed while she talked, her cheeks rosy and her eyes bright with affection.

Now he had to tear his eyes away from *her.* He had some more questions to ask and must not appear too personally interested in the answers. "Have the authorities given you temporary custody of the baby?"

"Yes." He could hear the satisfaction in her voice.

"Just like that?"

"Just like that. I've got a good friend in Social Services."

The hell you say.

"Besides, good foster homes are hard to come by. Especially at such short notice."

He looked up again, his facial expression carefully controlled. "Is it typical for the foster mother to actually…um…*name* the child?"

Allie laughed and grabbed hold of the baby's tiny pink fist, which was poking out of the blanket. "It's better than just calling him 'the baby,' isn't it?"

Liam said nothing, but consoled himself with the thought that "Jake" would never remember being called by that name. In the meantime, Liam would think up something much more suitable than the shortened version of his grandmother's old flame! Cecil, maybe? Or perhaps Richard, after his own father.

Obviously Allie had completely ignored, or forgotten, his words to her in the office the night before…that he wanted to be involved in any and all decisions made about the baby. To remind her now would be a big mistake. In fact, he shouldn't have said anything like that in the first place. He had to come across as nonthreatening as possible.

Liam noticed that the bottle was half gone, so he slipped the nipple out of the baby's mouth and propped him in a sitting position in his lap, then slightly bent the baby at the waist and gently patted him on the back. In less than thirty seconds, the baby burped satisfactorily and Liam proceeded to give him the rest of the bottle.

"I'm impressed," Allie said. "Most men don't even know babies *need* burping, much less the proper way to do it."

"I've had practice," Liam said modestly. "I *am* a father, you know." He regretted that last statement. By association, it might remind Allie of his loss of Victoria and the baby a year ago.

There was an awkward pause, during which he supposed Allie was wondering whether or not to bring up the subject. He hoped she wouldn't. He never knew how to reply to people's polite expressions of condolence. Saying "thank you" was short and proper, but not something he enjoyed repeating over and over again. *Thank you.* Thank you for what?

"Jake's asleep," is what she finally said to break the silence. "Give him to me and I'll put him in the baby carrier for now. I've got a crib coming for him later."

Liam was perfectly capable of putting Jake in the baby carrier himself, but he didn't think he should be too pushy. He stood up and reluctantly handed the baby to Allie. As she bent over the carrier, he noticed a reddish spot on her crown where she'd made contact with the door frame.

"Good God, I think you're actually bleeding," he said. "Sit down and let me have a look at it. Have you got hydrogen peroxide?"

"Of course I do," she replied, a note of impatience in her voice. "I've got sutures and a needle, too. But I'm not going to let *you* sew me up if that's what's needed."

He shook his head at her. "I only want to look at

it, tell you what I see, clean it up a bit and perhaps cover it with a Band-Aid. You act as if I want to do brain surgery. If you need stitches—which I doubt, because you'd be bleeding more heavily—I'd be happy to accompany you to the hospital.''

She faced him, her hands on her slim hips. "What is it with you and hospitals? If I need suturing, my grandfather can do it. We pretty much try to take care of ourselves around here. And we don't like being ordered around.''

From Allie's attitude, Liam was getting a pretty good idea about the mind-set in Annabella. They were all probably a pretty independent bunch, and Allie one of the most independent.

Victoria was different. Victoria had relied on Liam. If he'd said "sit down and let me have a look at it,'' she'd have sat down, grateful that he wanted to take care of her. She wouldn't have misconstrued his intentions and accused him of ordering her around.

"You're one to complain about being ordered around,'' he found himself saying. "You're one of the bossiest women I've ever met.''

Up came her chin another notch. "If you're referring to last night, I find that comment incredibly ironic. You were complaining that I wasn't doing things fast enough…remember? Now you're suggesting that I should have said 'please' and 'thank you' and been more demure, I suppose?''

Suddenly Liam could see how ridiculous he was being. Not to mention rude and ungentlemanly. His father and grandfather would be appalled. Hell, *he* was appalled. What was it about Allie Lockwood—besides the fact that she stood in the way of something he wanted desperately—that pushed all his buttons?

"I'm sorry, Allie. I'm being rude. And I was rude last night. I had a better excuse for it then, but that doesn't entirely absolve me. I'm grateful for all you did last night and I have complete faith in your abilities as a doctor. I'll try to be more of a gentleman."

Allie's hands slipped off those lovely hips of hers. "How do you do that? How do you make me mad as the dickens one minute, then pop my bubble of indignation in the next? Did it ever occur to you that I just might *like* staying mad at you for more than a minute?"

Liam had no idea how to reply to this complex, and rather gratifying, question, and was saved the attempt when the doorbell rang. It was the second time that day he'd been "saved by the bell." Instead of answering it immediately, however, Allie continued to stare up at Liam with a truly puzzled expression in her dark brown eyes. He decided that puzzlement suited her, flattered her. Maybe because it showed a softer, more vulnerable side to the indomitable Doctor Lockwood. Not to mention the fact that she had very beautiful eyes...

"That will probably be his crib," she finally said.

Liam was surprised that a furniture store would deliver so late in the evening, but when Allie swung open the door, it was Doug Renshaw who was standing there holding a big oblong cardboard box under one arm. His eyes took in the sight of Allie in her pretty pink sweater and slim-fitting pants and a wide grin spread across his face. Liam decided then and there that Ribchester and Mrs. Preedy and the local gossip grapevine were right. Doug Renshaw was still in love with his ex-wife.

"Good, I'm glad you're here," Allie said brightly,

apparently unaware that she was probably encouraging her ex-husband to believe that it wasn't just the crib she was happy to see. But a desperately in-love man will take encouragement from just about anything, so maybe it wasn't all her fault.

"I still have to put it together. Might take a couple of hours," he was saying as he angled the box into the room. "Or maybe longer, I don't know—" Suddenly he saw Liam and his grin disappeared faster than the Cheshire Cat.

"We meet again, Sheriff," Liam said amiably.

"Hello...Mr. McAllister." Doug Renshaw could barely choke out the greeting. He wouldn't call him by his first name, as Liam requested they all do, but he had no intention of calling him Lord Roderick, either. Their meeting that morning had been tense and unnecessarily contentious. Liam had had to remind the sheriff more than once that *he* wasn't the perpetrator of the crime, and that no one wanted the mystery surrounding the baby to be solved more than Liam himself.

ALLIE LOOKED from her ex-husband's face to Liam's and back again. For some reason, those two didn't like each other. Doug got jealous easily—even though he didn't have the right to—but it was ridiculous for him to be jealous of Liam McAllister, a man who probably didn't look twice at anyone who wasn't at least a third cousin to the Queen. And beautiful. Don't forget *that*. Judging by her pictures, Victoria had been very beautiful.

Allie put a stop to the idle meanderings of her mind and asked Doug, "What have you found out? I assume you and Liam met earlier in the day to discuss the case. Were you able to come up with some clues?''

Doug leaned the box against the wall and sat down in what had always been his favorite chair. He looked tired. For the first time it occurred to Allie that Doug's dedication to this case might be due to something more than his considerable sense of duty. That he, too, had felt the cruel irony of someone throwing away a baby when they had tried so hard to bring one into the world. Her heart filled with sympathy…but she dared not show it. Doug was too easily encouraged.

While she and Liam waited for Doug to begin, in one unplanned coordinated movement they both sat down again on the couch. And because of all the room the baby carrier was taking up, only a couple of inches separated them. Doug observed this close proximity and got that glowering and sulky look on his face that Allie so disliked. But she wasn't about to pander to him by moving to another seat. Even if Liam's thigh was just an inch or two away…

Finally Doug spoke. ''I found out from Mr. Mc-Allister this morning that when he stopped at the Gas 'n Go last night, the door to the women's rest room was shut and locked.''

''I didn't know whether it was locked or jammed,'' Liam interjected. ''I couldn't open it.''

''When Lamont and I arrived at the scene, the door was open.''

Allie nodded. ''So you think the woman who gave birth to Jake was still in the bathroom when Liam showed up?''

''Yes.''

''And there's no doubt that she *did* give birth in that bathroom?''

Allie could see the slight disgusted curl of Doug's upper lip. "No doubt. In fact there was so much blood, I was sure she'd need medical attention or might even end up dead. But I checked at the hospital and the morgue and no female was admitted to either in the last twenty-four hours. I'll check again tomorrow, and for the next few days if necessary."

"So where do you go from here, Doug?" Allie asked. "Without any suspects, the DNA evidence won't do you any good."

Doug ran an open palm down the side of his face, then grabbed the back of his neck. It was a gesture Allie was familiar with. She used to knead those tight neck muscles for him. "You're right. We can't take DNA from everyone within a hundred-mile radius, then compare."

"And you're sure it wasn't someone just passing through?" Liam suggested.

"Pretty sure. Eighty percent sure. Not many people pass through this part of Utah. We're definitely out of the way of the freeways and main roads."

"But whoever stopped at the Gas 'n Go to have her baby didn't get there on foot," Allie said, thinking out loud. "And if she was still there when Liam showed up—"

Doug smiled his approval. "You think more and more like a law officer, Allie. I guess your five years with me weren't completely wasted."

Embarrassed, Allie shot a quick glance at Liam. Doug took every opportunity to refer to their marriage, especially in front of other men. But Liam had turned his head and was tucking Jake's blanket around his tiny feet.

When Allie had nothing to say to Doug's comment,

he continued. "I checked with Bob Johnson and he said there were three vehicles parked at the station, one for a carburetor rebuild and two for inspections. A Taurus, a Camry and an '85 Ford truck."

He looked pointedly at Liam. "I was hoping Mr. McAllister could tell me what vehicles he saw at the station, and by the process of elimination we'd know what make and model had been driven there by the baby's mother."

Liam shook his head regretfully. "I circled the station looking for a phone booth, but I was so panicked about getting the baby to a doctor I just barely remember seeing those parked cars at the station. I recall seeing the truck, but that's the only one that stands out in my mind."

"Since Mr. McAllister distinctly recalls only the one truck at the scene, it seems likely that the fourth vehicle was another sedan, which doesn't really narrow it down much." Doug threw Liam another baleful glance. "It would help a lot if Mr. McAllister had a better memory."

"Considering the circumstances, Doug, you can't fault him for that," Allie quickly put in. Doug just wasn't being fair!

Her ex just shrugged and said nothing. It was another gesture she recognized.

"What about the quilt Liam told you about?"

"It's the one piece of evidence that might take us somewhere," Doug admitted. "If someone can identify even one or two patches of fabric, we could maybe figure out who made the quilt."

"Not to be pessimistic," Allie warned, "but the problem with that idea is that we've had quilting bees here since Annabella was settled."

She turned to Liam. "Women bring all their fabric pieces together and put them in a communal pile. They get more variety that way. Everyone picks fabric pieces out of that pile."

She turned back to Doug. "The only way a fabric identification would be helpful is if the quilt was made at home by someone using only their own fabric pieces. Besides, this quilt was old and tattered, right? It's probably an heirloom, made by someone's grand-mother."

"That's why I've got Irma Tait calling all her quilt-making buddies to a meeting tomorrow night at the office," Doug said. "The place will be chock-full of old ladies, and I'm hoping just one of them will be able to identify the quilt as belonging to some family or other, or maybe just identify the fabric pieces as having once been someone's homemade Sunday dress or apron, or whatever."

Allie leaned forward, her hands clasped and resting on her knees. "It's a good plan, Doug. It's a start, anyway. But what will you do if this leads to a dead end? How long do you plan to look for Jake's biolog-ical mother?"

Doug didn't hesitate. "I plan to exhaust every means in my power and look as long as it takes."

Doug's determination sent a chill down Allie's spine. She'd never really believed they'd find the mother. Now she wasn't so sure.

Doug apparently saw and understood Allie's reac-tion and said in a much gentler tone, "That doesn't mean the baby—that Jake—can't be put up for adop-tion after the time period required in abandonment cases, Allie. A mother who'd throw away her baby like that doesn't deserve a second chance, anyway."

Allie nodded, her eyes on the carpet.

"Really, Allie, I don't think you've got anything to worry about."

Allie looked up, aware that Liam was watching and listening. "Who told you I had long-term plans for Jake?"

Doug shook his head, a sad, wistful smile on his handsome face. "I *know* you, Allie. I know how you think…and what you've been through. Besides, what woman names a baby after their grandfather with plans to give him away?"

Turning to Liam, Allie said hesitantly, "Well…now you know."

Liam met her gaze squarely. "I already knew. Maybe I don't have a past relationship to give me insight into your personality, but anyone seeing you with the baby could have easily figured out what your intentions are."

"So, I'm that transparent," Allie said with a sigh. "I don't know why, but I feel kind of shy about this…like I just announced that I was pregnant."

"Well I, for one, think it's great," Doug said warmly.

Allie waited, but Liam said nothing.

HE KNEW he was disappointing Allie by not climbing aboard her adoption bandwagon, but Liam couldn't stoop to that level of hypocrisy. He was already more deeply mired in the muck than he wanted to be. Instead, he put a stop to all the sentimental claptrap going on by standing up and offering to help Doug put the crib together.

"What?" Doug exclaimed, clearly surprised…just

as Liam knew he would be. Surprised and none too pleased.

"With the two of us working on it, we could have it up in no time at all."

Obviously Doug had hoped to make the crib-building project last as long as possible. And even if he liked Liam, which he didn't, he didn't want help *or* company unless it was Allie's.

Enjoying Doug's tongue-tied displeasure, Liam couldn't resist adding, "I'm rather good with tools."

It looked for a minute as though Doug might tell Liam exactly what he could do with his tools, but everyone was saved that embarrassment when the doorbell sent another chime echoing through the house.

"Who could that be?" Allie mumbled as she headed for the door. Swinging it open, she exclaimed, "Gramps? What are you doing here?"

Chapter Five

Liam watched with interest as Dr. Jacob Lockwood, his grandmother's childhood sweetheart and a real American war hero, walked into the room. He did, indeed, have a slight limp, but looked very robust. He was tall and lanky, slightly stooped at the shoulders as if he'd bent over and listened to a lot of hearts through his stethoscope over the years, with a shock of thick white hair and deep-set brown eyes. He wore a Levi's jacket over a tan sweater, faded jeans and cowboy boots.

"You didn't think I could stay away after hearing that awful story about the baby in the Dumpster, and then found out from Kayla that suddenly I've got a namesake! Where is the little—"

He turned and saw Liam standing by the couch. He must have realized that Doug was there, too, and so was his "namesake," but he couldn't seem to take his eyes off Liam or utter another word. It was embarrassing to Liam, but he understood the old man's shock and curiosity. If his grandmother, Mary, hadn't jilted Jacob Lockwood for an amnesiac English lord,

Liam wouldn't even exist. Sizing up Liam was, in a way, like sizing up the man who had stolen his fiancé.

"Gramps, this is Liam McAllister," Allie said in a halting voice, very unlike her usual confident tone. She was obviously sensitive to how her grandfather was feeling and wasn't sure what to expect next.

"I know who he is, Allie," Jacob said quietly. His eyes narrowed as he spoke directly to Liam. "I've seen your picture on the covers of those tabloid rags from time to time. Don't buy 'em, of course. Just see 'em in the checkout line over at the Safeway."

"Glad to hear you don't buy them, sir. I'm ashamed to be an occasional subject for their particularly loathsome form of journalism." He extended his hand. "I've heard a lot about you, sir, and am pleased to meet you."

"Heard a lot about me, eh?" Jacob looked down at Liam's outstretched hand for a moment, as if slightly perplexed. As if weird, unexpected things were happening to him and he wasn't sure how to respond. Then, to Liam's relief, Jacob took his hand in a firm grasp.

"I'm pleased to meet you, too, young man. I never thought I'd have the pleasure. Mary…er…your grandmother keeps to herself, and I'd have expected any visiting family to do the same."

"Well, chances are we might not have met if I hadn't made that stop at the petrol station last night," Liam admitted.

"Thank God you did," Jacob said. He turned and squinted down at the baby. "Looks as pink and healthy as a prize piglet…only a hell of a lot luckier."

"Yes, sir," Liam agreed.

Jacob turned back to Liam with a scowl. "Quit calling me 'sir,' if you don't mind. Makes me feel as old as Methuselah, or back in the Navy. My name's Jacob."

Liam smiled. "And my name's Liam. I'm trying to get everyone around here to call me that—" He flitted a glance toward Doug. "But I'm not having a whole lot of luck. Maybe if *you* set the example."

Jacob nodded. "No problem." He turned to Doug and nodded again…curtly. "Evenin', Sheriff."

"Hello, Doc." Doug sounded and looked melancholy, as if resigned to the fact that the house was filling up with far too many people to suit his purposes.

"Doug picked up a crib for me today and he's here to put it together," Allie explained in a hurried manner, as if feeling the need to justify Doug's presence to her grandfather. It appeared to Liam that there were some unresolved and probably bitter feelings between Jacob and Doug. But that was understandable if Doug was the cheating ex-husband he was rumored to be. "Liam's offered to help," Allie added.

"Well, I'm here to stay for awhile and am as good as the next guy at putting up a crib," Jacob said. "Two working together will make it go faster, though, so—"

Here it comes, thought Liam. Jacob was going to tell Doug to go home, that he wasn't needed. That he, Liam, could help Jacob put up the crib.

Jacob turned to Liam. "So, since you're here to visit your grandmother and she's probably waitin' up for you—not to mention you've got a daughter who's probably wantin' a bedtime story about now—feel free to go on home. I can help Doug put up the crib.''

To say the least, Liam was surprised. And, yes, offended. He'd been dismissed and reminded of his familial responsibilities as if he was a fourteen-year-old boy. Or maybe all that folksy niceness was just a front, and Jacob didn't like Liam any better than—or even as much as—he liked his granddaughter's cheating ex-husband.

Or maybe he didn't like Liam because of who he was…the grandson of Cecil McAllister. Maybe Gran's old sweetheart *did* hold a grudge.

On the other hand, maybe it wasn't personal at all. Since he was standing up when Jacob arrived, maybe he thought he had been on the verge of leaving, that he *wanted* to go home. And maybe Jacob sensed his granddaughter's tension and fatigue and was trying to help her out by emptying the room of at least one hovering male.

Liam looked at Allie. She'd said she hadn't slept much the night before, and he was sure she was eager to get the crib up and things in order, then get to bed for some much-needed rest. It was guaranteed that the baby…that *Jake*—he might as well call him that for the time being—would be getting her up in a couple of hours for another bottle and diaper change, anyway. The sooner she was left alone, the better.

Liam hadn't wanted to go before, and now he knew why. He suddenly realized that he felt much better about leaving Allie and the baby with her grandfather on the premises, rather than alone with Doug. Why he felt so much better, he wasn't sure. And he wasn't going to analyze it.

Ignoring Doug's victorious smirk, Liam smiled and said, "You're right. I need to go home. But be sure and look at the top of Allie's head before you leave tonight, Jacob. She's injured. In fact, I'd advise you to look at it before you start on the crib. And promise me you won't let her put you off, okay?"

Allie got pink in the face and Doug's smirk dissolved into a sulky scowl, but Jacob didn't seem the least bit annoyed by Liam's parting orders. He simply raised his brows, slid an amused look at the others, and said, "I'll do that, son. Good night now."

Liam got home just in time to read *Goodnight Moon* to a drowsy Bea and tuck her into bed. Later he had some tea and cake with his grandmother by the fire and told her about checking in on the baby at Allie's, but he didn't tell her about meeting Jacob Lockwood. He still wasn't sure exactly why Jacob sent him home. Until he knew for sure it had nothing to do with grudging feelings toward Mary, and any and all offspring of her union with an English lord, he'd keep their meeting to himself.

IT TOOK an extraordinary amount of willpower, but for the next four days Liam stayed away from Allie and little Jake. He kept tabs on them by sending Ribchester and Mrs. Preedy into town every day, ostensibly to obtain groceries, toiletries, etc., but really to collect gossip. The old couple loved these excursions, which had been too few and far between when only Mary was at the house.

Liam found out that Allie's younger sister, Kayla, was baby-sitting Jake during the day and, by all accounts, doing a great job. Jake was fine and showed no developmental problems as a result of his traumatic birth. As for the investigation, Doug's gaggle of quilting ladies had not been able to identify any of the squares of fabric on the small quilt that had been wrapped around Jake by his runaway mother.

In fact, Doug's investigation seemed to be going nowhere, but he wasn't about to give up. He wouldn't be satisfied till he'd done everything possible to find Jake's biological mother or father, or any other relative for that matter. However, he was determined to do it all himself, for which Liam was extremely grateful. By keeping the story contained locally, perhaps they'd avoid the media getting involved and finding out Liam's part in it. He did not want the town inundated by the paparazzi, making his life and everyone else's a living hell.

In the meantime, Liam's lawyer in California was boning up on state laws and international regulations related to adoption in Utah.

Liam spent those four days with Bea and his grandmother, the three of them taking walks in the woods, picnicking, playing card games and reading Bea's favorite books out loud. It should have been a relaxing, restoring time for Bea, but she still had little appetite, got tired very easily, and had a short attention span. Any attempts at drawing her out to talk about her mum were disastrous. Twice she ran away, crying. Liam was at his wit's end.

He thought about talking to Mary again about her

offhand suggestion that Jacob Lockwood might be able to help with Bea, but he was reluctant to bring up the subject when he wasn't sure how Jacob "stood" on their family.

On the fourth day of Liam's self-imposed exile from town and certain people in it, he asked Bea if she'd like to go to Annabella's centrally located park to play on the swings and maybe afterward get an ice cream cone. She responded with more enthusiasm than he'd seen for awhile, and that afternoon they set off in the Jeep. Gran had been invited—*entreated*—to go with them, but she had refused with a smile.

When they got to the park, Bea appeared excited at the sight of a few children enjoying the playground toys, but held back shyly. Liam bent down and whispered encouragement and finally she walked toward the running, laughing children to try and make a new friend or two.

Liam watched her timid advance with the full and aching heart of a parent. Oh, how much he wanted her to be happy! To be healthy! To get over her mother's passing and once again embrace life with joy and confidence and energy.

He held his breath till he saw Bea talking with another little girl with blond hair and pigtails, then the two of them walked together to the slide. Bea turned and flashed him a quick, delighted smile...and he could breathe again.

Liam looked around, planning to settle in till Bea was ready to go for that ice cream cone. He saw a bench where he could keep an eye on Bea, but it was partially occupied by a woman who was grasping the handles of a perambulator…or baby buggy, as the Americans called them. She was gently bouncing the buggy and crooning at the infant inside.

As it was the only empty spot and the best place from which he could observe the whole playground area, and since he had a certain fascination with babies lately, Liam approached the bench. He just hoped the woman wouldn't recognize him.

No such luck. As he came close enough to be recognized, the woman turned, stared, then smiled from ear to ear. "Liam McAllister! Where have you been keeping yourself? You've been in town nearly a week and you haven't come to see me."

Liam stopped in his tracks. "I'm terribly sorry, but do I know you?" he inquired politely. Lots of times people *thought* they knew him, simply because his face was familiar from all those rag sheet covers and media news stories about the English aristocracy.

The young woman, dressed in a navy-blue sweatshirt and sweatpants, her strawberry-blond hair a halo of curls around her plump but pretty face, continued to smile. "You *used* to know me. In fact, although you were always very kind to me, I'm sure you thought I was the biggest pest."

Now he was completely bewildered. Although, there was something familiar and attractive about her eyes.

"I'm Kayla, Allie's younger sister," she finally explained.

Liam was very glad to know who she was, although he was still puzzled by her reference to their having met before. He didn't remember ever meeting Kayla or thinking she was a pest. Today he was actually quite delighted to have accidentally met up with her, because if she was Kayla, the baby in the buggy had to be Jake.

Liam's heart beat faster as he took the last few steps to the bench and sat down. "I'm pleased to meet you," he said.

She laughed, throwing her head back and slanting a coy look at him. Yes, she definitely had those fascinating Lockwood eyes. Eyes like Allie's. Deep brown with long, thick lashes.

"But I told you, we've already met."

"Not recently, because surely I'd have remembered *you*," was his gallant reply…an automatic response after years of bantering with flirtatious women.

Kayla laughed again, and Liam tried to sneak a look at the baby. Jake appeared to be warmly bundled up and fast asleep. He could barely see the curve of one rosy little cheek. He supposed it would be a shame to wake him….

"Don't worry, Liam. I didn't really expect you to remember me. It was when you visited your grandmother twenty years ago. I was only five years old."

Even with this information, Liam couldn't for the life of him remember ever meeting Kayla.

"Do you remember the two boys who came up to your grandmother's place and played with you?" Kayla suggested helpfully. "Tom and Jerry?"

Liam laughed, those names coming back to him like a bolt out of the blue. "Yes! Tom and Jerry…like the cartoon cat and mouse."

"Yes, they're my brothers. And I was the little girl

who tagged along and got in the way as much as I possibly could.''

Staring at the ground, Liam let his mind return to that summer twenty years ago and the two weeks he'd spent with Mary in Utah. He'd just turned thirteen and was starved for some other guys to pal around with by the time Tom and Jerry worked up the courage to see if the British kid wanted to hang out with them.

He'd welcomed them wholeheartedly. They were slightly younger than him, but full of fun ideas of things to do and make and explore in the woods surrounding Mary's cabin.

And, come to think of it, he *did* remember a little girl.... She was a cherubic child with curly red hair and pale freckles, always carrying a doll or two and wanting to play "house." She tagged along persistently despite her brothers' frequent admonitions to "Go away, Kay! We don't want to play with you and your dolls!" Although she never seemed disheartened by her brothers' rejections; Liam remembered feeling sorry for her and occasionally doing little kind things for her.

"I can see by your expression you *do* remember me,'' Kayla said happily.

Liam looked up and smiled. "Yes, I do. I wonder I didn't remember before.''

"It was a long time ago.'' She looked down and kicked the dirt with the toe of her athletic shoe.

"But you were too little to walk up that hilly, private road by yourself. How'd you get there? I don't think your brothers brought you...at least not willingly.''

"No, my brothers wouldn't take me," Kayla admitted with a cheeky grin. "I hitched a ride with Allie on her bike. She didn't want to take me, either, but I pitched a fit and my mother made her."

"Allie was there, too?" Liam was surprised and chagrined. How could he have forgotten someone like Allie? Even as a child she must have been a force to be reckoned with.

"She was there, but she was hiding in the cottonwood tree, spying on us the whole time. She was too chicken to come down and meet you," Kayla said with a certain smug satisfaction. "Even though I know she thought you were cute."

Liam wasn't sure how to reply to this announcement. On the one hand he found the idea of the confident, strong-willed Allie hiding in a tree, too shy to come down, rather endearing. On the other hand, he thought Kayla's pleasure in revealing her sister's shyness all those years ago, rather immature.

As for Allie thinking he was "cute"… Well, that was twenty years ago, too.

"Your sister has never struck me as shy," Liam couldn't help commenting in a thoughtful tone.

"Oh no, she's not anymore," Kayla confirmed. "No siree. Allie pretty much goes after what she wants. And she always gets it, you know. *Always.*"

Liam studied what he could see of Kayla's averted face. He decided to risk prying a little. "You must be thinking about her plans to adopt Jake. About how she made up her mind so quickly, and is so determined and single-minded about the whole thing. And with her friends in Social Services, so far things seem to be working out very easily for her. Is that what you meant when you said Allie always gets what she wants?''

Kayla stared at him, surprise clearly showing on her face. ''Oh no. I wasn't thinking of that at all. But you're right, of course. Her decision to adopt Jake, and the fact that nothing and no one will stand in her way, is a perfect example of Allie always getting what she wants.''

Liam nodded, his curiosity aroused. He wondered if he dared ask one more prying question. ''Well then, what *were* you thinking of when you said Allie gets whatever she wants?''

Kayla shook her head wonderingly. ''Oh there's so many examples, really. But I was thinking about Doug. She decided she wanted Doug and she got him.'' She snapped her fingers. ''Just like that.'' Kayla slid Liam another coy smile. ''So, I'd watch out if I were you. Maybe it's *you* she wants now.''

Liam wasn't sure whether to laugh or not. Was Kayla teasing, or was she perfectly serious?

''Mommy! Mom*meeee!*''

Kayla's head snapped around and she sprang to her feet. ''Travis?''

Liam watched as Kayla hurried over to a little red-headed boy standing in a sandbox not five feet away. Now he remembered hearing that Kayla had a three-year-old son. And that he was a handful.

''Travis, why did you *do* that, honey?''

Travis had evidently not been the one calling to his mommy. Travis was the child standing over another little boy with a bucket of sand on his head. The other child was screaming bloody murder and a woman—undoubtedly his mother—was hurrying over to rescue him.

Liam observed the scene with sympathy for all involved. He couldn't hear what anyone was saying anymore because of the other child's loud crying, but it looked like Kayla was apologizing. Travis, on the other hand, stood with his arms crossed over his puffed-out chest and appeared unrepentant and vindicated. The other mother was grim-faced with the usual outrage parents feel for their picked-on children.

Liam could see that the little boy was unharmed, just a bit sandy, but he was milking the situation for all it was worth and his dry-eyed, indignant howls drowned out everything else being said or shouted. But he got the impression from Travis's gestures and facial expressions—when his mother apparently implored him to explain himself—that the other little boy had destroyed his sand fort, the crumbled proof of which was plain to see.

Liam was tending toward siding with Travis. And it looked like Kayla had grasped the true facts of the situation and was sticking up for him, too.

The noise finally woke up Jake. He started out whimpering, but quickly escalated to crying at the top of his lungs with little fists and feet flailing beneath his blanket. Jake looked at Kayla, observed that she was still deeply embroiled in the sandbox debacle, and decided that there was nothing else he could do but pick Jake up.

This he did with great satisfaction. And it was even more satisfying when Jake blinked open his eyes and stared fixedly at Liam, then suddenly quit crying. No bottle or diaper change was needed, apparently. At least, not just yet. For the moment Jake seemed satisfied to simply be held. Maybe—and Liam knew it was probably foolish to think so—Jake somehow remembered Liam's face and sensed his concern and love.

Liam held the baby and smiled down at him, charmed to his core, but not so charmed that he forgot his daughter. He looked up and scanned the playground, locating her still playing with the blond, pigtailed girl. But then he saw someone else. Someone walking purposely across the playground toward him. A slender, blond woman in a red sweater, a black skirt that skimmed her hips then flared midcalf, and tall black boots. It was Allie.

Never had Liam felt such conflicting emotions. Because he was holding Jake, he felt like a child caught with his hand in the cookie jar. But if Allie had suspected him of having intentions of his own concerning Jake, surely his recent absenteeism must have calmed those concerns. He hoped so. He hoped Allie was deceived into believing him a non-threat.

On the other hand, he felt awful about deceiving her and wished—suddenly wished quite fervently—that he and Allie had met under different circumstances. But that was foolish, too. As he often reminded himself, he and Allie were worlds apart. Apparently his brain had been listening to this valid argument, but his wildly beating heart had not. Judging by the way his skin was tingling and his blood was heating up, other parts of his body had also been inattentive.

He was thrilled to see her. He'd missed her as much as he'd missed Jake.

ALLIE WAS FEELING such a mix of emotions, she wasn't sure whether to run as fast as she could *away* from Liam McAllister, or as fast as she could *toward* him. She was jealous of him holding Jake. Running into him like this unexpectedly, seeing the look on his face as he gazed down at her baby, brought back the fears she'd felt that first night Liam brought Jake to the house.

On the other hand, the sight of him holding Jake made her yearn for a man in her life. Not just any man. Against her better judgment, it was Liam Mc-Allister she was suddenly yearning for. A man who could be autocratic and abrupt. A man who lived in another country, in another world, not just an ocean away but *oceans* away in terms of their backgrounds, lifestyles and futures. Why was she always attracted to the wrong guys? she wondered, her approach slowing as she drew near the bench.

When she was finally standing before Liam, she found herself appreciatively observing him in his burgundy sweater and tan pants, clean-shaven and with the autumn sun in his hair, and thinking, *It would be so great if we could just have a little fling while he's here. The memories of a fling with Liam McAllister would probably keep me going for several years. But he's probably not even attracted to me....*

"Hello, Allie."

Allie felt her face flood with warmth. It was a good thing he couldn't read her mind. She wondered how long she'd been standing there, not saying anything. She must have looked as moronic as she felt. *A fling? You mean an affair, don't you, Allie?* How irresponsible. How utterly impossible.

"Hello," she finally managed. "What are you doing here?"

"I brought Bea to play with the other children." He ducked his head to indicate a direction. "She's over there by the swings."

"Oh." Then it occurred to her, belatedly, that Kayla should be there. "But where are Kayla and Travis?" She looked around, saw Kayla in the sandbox, assessed what she saw and heard, and instantly understood. "Ah. I see Travis has caused a little ruckus."

"Yes, but I don't really think it's all his fault," Liam told her as he shifted Jake in his arms to a position perfect for taking a bottle. Jake had begun to whimper, his way of saying he was hungry, and Liam had understood immediately. "I've been watching, and I think Travis was just protecting his turf, so to speak. The other little boy ruined his fort or castle or whatever he was building."

Allie nodded, watched as Liam helped himself without asking to a bottle in Jake's buggy. Just before popping it into Jake's mouth—which was already puckered up and waiting—Liam looked at Allie. "Do you mind?"

Although it still troubled her when she watched Liam feeding or holding or interacting in any way with Jake, Allie felt it would be ridiculous to object. She nodded absently, amazed that she could be so spellbound by the paternal scene before her while, at the same time, feeling so anxious.

She reverted to their original subject. "Travis is full of energy and personality…sometimes a little *too* much. He gets pretty wild and hyper, especially in the evenings. I think he might have A.D.D."

This comment seemed to catch Liam's attention. "So you've been trained to recognize these sorts of disorders in children?"

"Yes, but I'm careful not to go beyond my abilities. I send many of the children I suspect of having emotional problems to a psychologist for evaluation, but there are some that simply need a little bit of listening to. Sometimes it's an obvious chemical imbalance and I try medications on a limited, very controlled trial run, then send them to Dr. Spendlove in Kamas if they aren't responding."

"How do you know which ones to send and which ones to work with first?"

Allie observed Liam closely. Was he testing her, doubting her again? Or was there another reason for his questions?

"I know most of my patients pretty well," she answered carefully. "I have good instincts. And I've done my homework. But I do have a wonderful resource here in Annabella. Someone I call in as a consultant, so to speak."

"And who might that be?" By the twinkle in his eyes and the faint smile that curved his lips, Allie saw that Liam had already guessed the answer.

Allie smiled back. "Yes, it's my grandfather. He's wonderful with children and has a great ability to figure them out and help them work through their problems. If he hadn't been a small-town GP, he'd have made a wonderful pediatrician, or pediatric psychologist for that matter.''

Liam's smile slipped away and he looked suddenly thoughtful. ''Your grandfather,'' he repeated, as if to himself.

She cocked her head to the side. ''Why are you so curious?''

He glanced past Allie toward the children playing on the toys, then down at Jake. ''No special reason, really.''

Allie believed that answer about as much as she believed in the Tooth Fairy. She had instantly thought of Bea, but she knew this was not the right time to bring up the possibility that Liam had some concerns about his daughter. Considering what the child had gone through just a year ago, Allie wouldn't be at all surprised if Bea was having some emotional problems. And by the frail look of her, the emotional problems were affecting her physical well-being.

''Allie! You're here! I thought you were coming to the house at five-thirty!''

Flushed and looking nervous and exhausted, Kayla approached with Travis firmly in tow. Travis's lip was sticking out like the prow of a ship.

''My last patient cancelled, and I got through earlier than I expected to, anyway,'' Allie said. ''I was driving to your house and I saw you. Well, actually, I saw Liam holding Jake.''

Kayla wiped her moist upper lip. ''Oh, and I'm *so* glad he was here. Although I'm sure I could have managed, anyway." Travis was tugging on her hand, trying to pull away. Kayla tousled his hair and bent down to give him a noisy kiss on his freckled cheek. A reluctant grin curved his lips. "I had to play sandbox referee, but Jake was fast asleep and in full view of—"

"Don't worry, Kayla, I understand. Why don't we—"

Suddenly a little blond-haired girl with pigtails appeared at Liam's elbow. "Are you that little girl's daddy?" she asked, pointing in the direction of the swings. "I think she's sick or something."

Allie turned and saw Bea sitting in the grass, leaning against one of the swingset poles. Even from a distance, Allie saw how pale she was. And her eyes were closed. In the same instant, Liam handed Jake to her and was running across the playground toward his daughter. Allie put Jake in the buggy and quickly followed.

Chapter Six

When Liam reached Bea, he knelt down and gently took hold of her shoulders. He silently thanked God when she opened her eyes and looked at him.

"What's the matter, Bea? Did you fall out of the swing? Are you hurt?" He looked her over quickly. She was very pale, but there were no obvious injuries.

"I'm all right, Daddy," Bea said with a tremulous smile. "I didn't hurt myself. I just didn't feel like playing anymore, so I sat down." Her eyes were brimming with tears, ready to spill over at the next blink.

He cupped her small face with both hands. "Oh, Bea—"

Suddenly Allie was there. She knelt down beside Liam and balanced herself with an open palm on his thigh. Startled, he glanced at her and was touched by her expression of concern as she observed his daughter. Obviously, she didn't even realize her hand was on his leg.

"Tell us what's wrong, Bea," Allie said. "If you didn't hurt yourself, are you sick? Did someone hurt your feelings?"

Bea closed her eyes and shook her head, making the tears spill over and run down her face. "No. Everyone's been nice. And I don't think I'm sick. I don't feel like throwing up or anything. I...I just got real tired all of a sudden." She looked up, her expression heartbreaking. "Can we go home, Daddy?"

"Of course, Bea. Come on, sweetheart, I'll carry you." Liam began to gather Bea into his arms.

"I have a better idea, Liam," Allie said, stopping him with a tentative touch to his shoulder. "Why don't you bring Bea to my house?"

Liam's first instinct was to immediately refuse. What was she thinking? Bea needed to feel safe and warm at home. But the look in Allie's eyes conveyed the impression that she had a specific reason for asking them to come to her house. Then Liam understood. Allie wanted to examine Bea. Liam wasn't sure why he hadn't thought of it himself.

"You're right," he said. "That *is* a better idea."

"But Daddy, I want to see Gran," Bea complained.

"You will see Gran. But first don't you want to see the baby we rescued the other night?"

Bea wiped away another plump teardrop wending its way down her cheek and visibly perked up. "Really, Daddy? I can see the baby? Can I hold it?"

Liam looked at Allie, got a quick nod of approval, then said to Bea, "Sure, you can hold him, but I might have to help you a little, okay?"

Bea was obviously eager to agree to any conditions that would enable her to hold Jake. Liam would use that eagerness to serve his purposes. He would make sure Bea had an examination by Allie in exchange for the coveted cuddling of little Jake.

TWO HOURS LATER, Allie stood with Liam in the doorway between her living room and dining room, both of them silently observing the sleeping children. Bea was curled up on the couch under a thick afghan. Jake was in his baby carrier on the floor. As dusk fell outside, a single lamp illuminated the darkening room. It was a very peaceful scene, but had been preceded by a lot of activity.

Allie had dropped off Kayla and Travis at their place, which was only two blocks away from the park, then drove home with Jake. Liam followed in his vehicle with Bea. Once they got inside the house, their first order of business had been to make sure the children were comfortable. Jake had just had a bottle, so all he needed was a diaper change. Thinking Bea's blood sugar might be low and contributing to her fatigue and melancholy, Allie got her some orange juice and a couple of pieces of string cheese.

Since Bea was only interested in holding Jake, it was difficult to get her to eat, but they finally succeeded by telling her that she had to be strong to hold Jake, and the juice and cheese would make her muscles grow.

While Bea had her refreshments, Liam called Mary and explained the situation in a hushed voice over the phone, and then called the one and only delivery service in Annabella, Rosie's Italian Restaurant, for pasta and salad. He explained to Allie that he wasn't sure how long he and Bea would be trespassing on her, and he didn't want her going to any extra trouble in the kitchen. Besides he was hungry, and he was hoping Bea would be hungry, too, once she got the baby-holding event out of her system.

Allie was agreeable to the plan. She was hungry, too. She had had a busy, if not long, day at the office, and had skipped lunch.

With Liam supporting the baby's head and generally supervising, Bea held Jake for some fifteen minutes. She giggled and smiled and cooed like a little mother-in-the-making the whole time, then she was reminded of her promise to allow Allie to look her over and submitted to the examination with only one beleaguered sigh. Afterward she was hungry enough to eat a small serving of pasta and a few forks of salad before nearly nodding off in the chair. Liam laid her down on the couch and she'd gone out like a light.

"Well, I guess we can finish our own dinners now," Liam said with a sigh. "I hope you don't mind if we stick around a little longer. I'd kind of like to let her sleep for awhile before taking her home. She might wake up and she looks so peaceful."

Allie and Liam were leaning against opposite door-jambs, just inches apart. Liam had taken off his sweater and folded up the sleeves of a long-sleeved white shirt to just below his elbows. His forearms were lean and muscular, the dark hair fine and soft-looking. His open collar revealed a strong column of neck and a triangle of smooth chest. Allie was standing close enough that she could see the pulse at the base of his throat and smell his musky aftershave. He needed another shave already. His five-o'clock shadow had arrived right on time and looked very sexy.

This leisurely perusal of Liam had not gone unnoticed. When their eyes met, there was a look in his that made Allie immediately straighten up and move away. Caught in the act, she felt herself blushing. "Yes, let's finish eating, and then we can talk about Bea," she said nervously.

She hurried into the kitchen and Liam followed. "You wouldn't happen to have any wine in the house, would you?" he asked her. "I'm tired as hell, but wound up, too. A little wine might ease the tension somewhat."

Which tension are you talking about? Allie wondered. *The sexual tension, or worry about Bea? Or both?* Speaking for herself, she could definitely vouch for feeling a little of both. No, that wasn't true. She was feeling a *lot* of both. However, she had no idea from which kind of tension Liam was suffering.

"I do have some wine." Standing in the middle of the kitchen with a reassuring six feet of distance between them, she turned and smiled. "It's not top of the line, though, which I'm sure is what you're used to."

Allie's comment made Liam grimace. Standing there with his hands on his slim hips and a slight slump in his wide shoulders, Allie could just imagine how tense those shoulder muscles were and longed to massage them.

"Please don't do that, Allie," Liam said wearily.

Allie nearly jumped. *Do what? Could he read her mind?*

"Believe me, I've had my share of cheap wine. I can't tell you how tired I am of people assuming I'm some fussy, stuck-up rich guy because I have a title. Just treat me like anyone else you might share a drink and some dinner with."

Allie understood Liam's dilemma—and she was glad he hadn't read her mind the moment before—but she wondered how on earth she was supposed to treat him like anyone else. After all, he *was* the famous, handsome, titled Liam McAllister, and he *was* rich. Maybe he wasn't stuck-up, though. Allie would allow him time to prove himself on that one.

"Hey, who said the wine was cheap?" she teased, trying to lighten the mood. "I just said it wasn't top of the line."

He responded with a smile, and she felt amply rewarded. "Sit down. The pasta's getting cold. I'll get the wine."

She was glad she actually had a chilled bottle in the fridge and poured some into a couple of wine goblets and brought them to the table.

After a few bites of food and a few sips of wine, Allie could feel herself relaxing and saw the gradual easing of tension in Liam, too. But she was going to wait till he was ready to talk about Bea instead of bringing it up herself.

Finally he leaned back in his chair, one shoulder at a slant, his arm resting on the table, his long, elegant fingers loosely circling the bowl of the wine goblet. He leveled an earnest look at her and said, "Tell me about Bea."

Allie pushed back from the table, too, and avoided

his gaze by keeping her own eyes fixed on the task of folding her napkin in her lap, then refolding it. "Physically she's fine. A little too thin for her height and age, but she hasn't got any signs of disease that would warrant further testing."

Liam said nothing for a minute and Allie waited in suspense. Surely he knew, as she did, what the real problem was. Finally he said, "I'm relieved to hear that, although I'm not really surprised. She's had a lot of colds and different kinds of viruses over the past year—"

"Since her mother died?" Allie looked up. She was determined to quit being a coward and address the real issue here, even if the subject was painful to Liam. Bea's health was at stake.

He met her gaze, but she saw so much repressed pain in his eyes, her heart ached for him. "Yes. Since her mother—and her little brother—died. I've taken her to a couple of therapists, but she wouldn't talk to either of them. She won't talk to me, either. Not about her mum, anyway. Part of the time she seems okay, but, like I said, she gets sick so frequently, and she just seems to be getting thinner as the weeks pass. She's easily distracted, loses interest quickly in even her favorite activities. Can't walk or play for very long without getting tired. Today was worse than usual, though. Maybe the added stress of meeting new friends did her in." He shook his head. "I don't know, Allie. I just don't know."

Allie nodded, empathizing with his feelings of helplessness. "Bea is depressed. Depression suppresses the immune system. In fact, studies have shown that depression can even make adults more susceptible to heart disease and other serious illnesses. It's just not good for you.''

Liam spread his hands wide. ''But what can I do? If she won't talk to anyone…''

''Have you tried medications?''

''A couple. One of them made her sleep all the time, the other gave her insomnia. I know there's a whole bunch more we could try, but even if they helped, I'd still feel better about it if she could talk about what's bothering her and deal with her feelings. I thought maybe a change of scenery would help.''

''So that's why you came to Utah?''

''Yes. I came for Bea. Although Gran thought it would do us both good.''

Liam settled into his former position, one hand idly caressing the stem of the wineglass, his expression reflective as he stared down at the table. Allie kept quiet and waited till he was ready to speak again.

Suddenly he looked up, smiling ruefully. ''The hell of it is, it's ended up helping *me*. Not Bea. I've only been here a few days, but I'm starting to feel better. You'll think I'm crazy, but being instrumental in saving Jake's life really made me feel like living mattered again.''

Allie raised her brows, a question implied but not spoken.

''No, I don't mean I didn't feel like life mattered before,'' he quickly clarified. ''I've got Bea. I love her more than anything. And I've got lots of people and things and hopes and dreams to live for, but I realized that I've been walking around for the past year like

some kind of zombie.'' He shook his head. "No wonder Bea's like she is."

Instinctively she reached over and laid her hand on
his. "Don't blame yourself. It isn't your fault. Besides,
what did you expect? Grief has its own timetable."

Liam's gaze fastened on her hand. Suddenly self-
conscious, Allie started to draw her hand away, but
Liam caught it and held fast. "That's what I told
Gran," he said. "But she thinks I've been grieving
too long, and she's probably right. She thinks I should
be dating again."

Allie's heart was starting to beat way too fast. Just
the chaste, simple contact of Liam's beautiful fingers
wrapped around hers was unnerving her, like she was
thirteen years old. "You…you haven't been dating?"

"Not at all. I haven't had the slightest inclination,
to be honest."

Allie gently tugged at her hand and he let go. "That
must be a disappointment to the media," she joked
weakly.

He finally looked up and an adolescent-like shyness
enveloped her again. "I'm not sure. They seem to take
equal delight in portraying me as either a playboy or
a tortured soul, destined never to give my heart away
again."

"But that's not you?"

"No, I have no desire to spend the rest of my life
like some Charlotte Brontë hero, holed away in a
dank, stone mansion on some blighted moor. I want
to marry again. I've never been happier than when I
was married. I want a family. I want more children.
Several. You can't imagine how wonderful it's been

holding Jake and experiencing those feelings of a new father again.''

Liam suddenly stopped talking, as if he realized he'd said too much already. And, selfishly, Allie was glad he'd stopped. Although it was gratifying that he felt comfortable enough to talk to her about private and painful feelings he might have been keeping pent-up for months, such revelations were bringing up painful feelings of her own.

Marriage. Family. Children. All things she wanted, too. She'd failed at marriage and she'd never bear her own children. But she did have Jake, she reminded herself, and nothing and no one would ever take him away from her.

It still made her anxious when Liam talked so lovingly of Jake, though. She knew he wasn't any threat, that he was just borrowing a little peace and joy from the simple act of holding and caring for an infant whose life he'd saved, but the affinity they had for each other was obvious. Jake was just a baby, but he quieted easily in Liam's arms. The affection seemed, somehow, a two-way thing.

And Bea seemed to love Jake, too. Allie had never seen Bea more animated than during those fifteen minutes when she held Jake in her arms.

Again it was brought home to Allie that Jake was a miracle. He was helping cure broken hearts. Liam's and maybe, in a smaller way, Bea's. As for herself, except for acquiring the always alert ear of a parent at night, she was sleeping better than she had in months. The baby dreams were gone. She didn't need them anymore. She had Jake.

"My ramblings seem to have sent you into a trance. Or have you dozed off with your eyes closed?"

Liam's wry comment stirred Allie from her musings. "I'm sorry. I wasn't bored at all. I was just thinking about what you were saying."

More than that, Liam's confessions had awakened her to reality again, given her a much-needed mental kick in the pants. While she and Liam had the same hopes and dreams for their futures—marriage, family and children—by what means those hopes were realized and those dreams came true would be vastly different from each other.

Liam would find himself a young, beautiful, *fertile* bride and have heirs by the dozens. Well, maybe not by the dozens, but certainly all they wanted.

Allie would have Jake and maybe another adopted child down the line, if she was lucky. Perhaps a little girl. And, as a single, working mother, she'd raise them in a home nothing like the traditional one she'd always imagined, but one just as good, just as wonderful, because it would be filled with love.

Having talked herself into a more sane and contented state of mind, she asked with a cheerful smile, "Are you up for some dessert?"

At first he looked puzzled at the abrupt change of subject, then his expression relaxed, as if he perfectly understood her. "Sure. I imagine you're tired of such serious topics. But first, do you mind if I thank you for listening to me?"

Allie smiled, shrugged. "If you want to. But it wasn't a big deal."

"It was to me."

"I'm glad I was here, then."

"So am I. But I hope this isn't the end of things."

Allie's heart skipped a beat. "What do you mean?"

"I still don't know what to do about Bea. I'd like your advice."

Allie felt guilty. She'd been thinking only of herself when Liam expressed a hope of not "ending things." He'd been talking about Bea, of course. For a moment there, she'd just about forgotten about that poor little girl. However, she did have definite ideas about what to do about Bea, but she wasn't sure how receptive Liam would be to them.

He saw her wheels turning, evidently, and had guessed her thoughts. "You think I ought to have your grandfather try and talk to her, don't you?"

"I do."

"And you're wondering if I've got some reason *not* to want him to talk to her. A reason related to my grandmother."

"Of course I am." She picked up her plate and carried it to the sink, then turned and faced him. "You and I have never discussed this before, so I'm assuming you know the whole story?"

He, in turn, brought his plate to the sink and stood disconcertingly close again. "I know what my grandmother told me. As for the whole story, I imagine I'd have to hear your grandfather's side of it, too."

"I don't think Gramps has any bad feelings toward Mary, if that's what you're wondering."

"Well, I didn't get that impression, either, when I met him the other day. But when he dismissed me to go home instead of your ex-husband, when I had the distinct impression that he didn't really *like* your ex-husband—''

Allie laughed. ''Gramps has a unique relationship with Doug. He tries not to like him, but he does anyway.''

''Do you have the same dilemma?'' Liam asked.

Allie was sobered by the question. Why was he asking it? ''Yes, I like Doug, despite everything,'' she answered honestly. ''But I have to be careful about *liking* him, because he gets encouraged easily. It would be easier if I hated him.''

Liam nodded. ''I see.''

By the expression in his eyes, Allie wasn't sure he did see. But she didn't want to talk about Doug.

''Does Mary hate Gramps?''

''Oh, no,'' Liam answered quickly and decisively. ''Not at all. Gran has only nice things to say about him.''

Allie went back to the table to pick up the silverware, but was really more concerned with putting distance between her and Liam. ''Then why does she stay holed up in that cabin? Why doesn't she come to town?''

Liam followed and helped clear the table. ''I think she feels guilty. I think she's still sorry for hurting your grandfather.''

They were back at the sink, side by side. ''Well, she *did* hurt him. But he got over it. He married my grandmother and they were very happy together. And I gather Mary was happy with your grandfather, too.'' She looked up at him. ''Right?''

"Yes."

"So why can't they be friends?"

"I don't know, Allie. When you hurt someone you love, or let them down in a terrible way, the guilt can be overwhelming."

By the painful and faraway look that suddenly came into Liam's eyes, Allie wasn't so sure he was talking about Mary and Jacob anymore. It occurred to her suddenly that he might somehow feel responsible for his wife's death. But that would be ridiculous. She'd read that Victoria McAllister had had toxemia. But it was definitely time to bring the focus of the conversation back to Bea.

She turned to face the room, leaned against the counter, and crossed her arms. "Well, whether they ever become friends again is up to them," she said with a note of finality. "It's really none of my business. But I know Gramps would be thrilled to help Bea if he could. He's not the type of man to hold grudges, or let his personal feelings in any way prejudice him against a defenseless child."

Liam moved to stand directly in front of her. *Why did he stand so close?*

"And I know my grandmother wouldn't object," he said. "And even if she did object, I'd have to think of Bea first. Will you talk to Jacob for me, Allie? See how soon he can start having sessions—or whatever he wants to call them—with Bea?"

His apparent respect for her advice was gratifying and touching. She couldn't help smiling up at him warmly. "I'm so glad you're trusting Gramps to do this. I really feel you won't be disappointed."

He smiled back, his green eyes even more attractive without the dark circles under them. He looked much more rested lately. Apparently Utah *did* agree with him. "I'm going on two very good recommendations. Yours and Gran's."

"I can understand your trusting your grandmother's judgment, but why mine?" she teased. "You didn't think much of my abilities that first night."

He made a playful grimace. "Please don't hold my behavior that night against me, Allie. I was in a panic, and jet-lagged on top of that. I apologize."

She waved an airy hand. "You've already apologized once. Don't worry about it."

He seemed to suddenly think of something. "How's your head? Did Jacob have to put a stitch in it?"

"Well, actually, he did," she admitted reluctantly. "But just one."

"Let me see."

"No. Really, it's okay."

But he'd already taken her face in his large hands, much the way he'd held Bea's small face with such tenderness on the playground. "Now tip your head and let me look," he urged her gently.

Allie felt she had no choice but to obey. And why shouldn't she? she asked herself. He was being so kind, so sweet, so—

"Ah, I see it. I should never have surprised you in the garage. Poor darling."

Darling?

Liam bent down and kissed the top of Allie's head. Like earlier when they'd briefly held hands, the touch was so chaste and simple, but his closeness, his kindness, his scent, was sending her senses reeling.

The kiss was over, but he still held her face in his hands, and now he slowly tilted her head till she was looking into his eyes. What she saw there took her breath away. Was it possible that he was as attracted to her as she was to him?

"You're so lovely, Allie," he whispered, his fingers threading through the hair at her temples, his low-pitched, husky voice like a caress. His eyes were mesmerizing. And his touch— His touch was heaven.

"Liam—" she started to protest weakly. But she couldn't help herself. Her arms came up and wrapped around his neck. She pulled him close. Or did he pull *her* close? It didn't matter.

Their lips touched and Allie felt a searing thrill of desire ripple through her body. The kiss started with a tentative respect on his part. There was a question in it. She answered the question by kissing him back with an eagerness that surprised her *and* him.

He pulled her close against his hard chest, and she felt pliant and sensitized. His hands began to roam her back, and hers to roam his.

Ah, it had been too long. But, on the other hand, it had never been like *this* before.... For Allie this was the first time she'd experienced such strength and suddenness of passion in a man's arms.

Oh my God, she thought. *I'm going to go to bed*

with this man I barely know. And I don't care. I want to. I want—

Jake began to cry. At first they pretended they didn't hear. At first neither of them seemed to want to return to reality. But slowly, reluctantly they stopped kissing and just held each other for a moment as their breathing slowly returned to normal. Then Liam held her at arm's length and they looked, astonished, into each other's eyes.

"God, Allie, I feel like I should be apologizing again. You must think I'm a real jerk, coming in here and giving you a sob story, then putting the moves on you."

She shook her head firmly and gave a rueful smile. "I don't think that at all. And I'm not sure who put the moves on who just now. We're both adults, Liam. There was nothing wrong with it…was there?"

Liam smiled back. "No, I guess not."

But Liam knew better. There was plenty wrong with it. He had no business kissing Allie. He had intentions of disrupting her happy little world and shouldn't be giving in to his attraction to her.

Yes, he had to finally admit it. He was attracted to Allie. *Incredibly* attracted to the one woman in the world he shouldn't be attracted to, all things considered. Hell, it wasn't fair to her and it wasn't the smartest and kindest thing he could do for himself, either.

As she slipped away and went to Jake, he watched her go with an ache in his heart and a feeling of foreboding. She was beautiful and passionate and tempting, but the wisest thing he could do would be to stay away from her completely. But now that he'd arranged for Bea to meet with Allie's grandfather, there would have to be *some* interaction between them.

Liam's hopes were high that Dr. Jacob Lockwood could help his little girl, and he'd be damned if he'd allow his libido to screw that up for her!

He walked into the living room. Allie had Jake on the couch, changing his diaper. She leaned over him and spoke in the low, soothing tones of a mother. Liam's heart felt like a clenched fist. Guilt consumed him. Guilt over his conduct with Allie and the secrets he kept from her. Guilt over Victoria and their lost child. Victoria should be leaning over their infant son, just as Allie was doing. Maybe if he'd been there when she got sick instead of in Germany at an art auction, Victoria and their baby would still be alive.

"Daddy?"

Bea was sitting up, sleepy-eyed and rosy. He turned to her.

"Hi, sweetheart. Have a good nap?"

"Yes, but can we go home now?"

"Yes, Bea, let's go home." He picked her up.

Allie turned and smiled. "I'll call you and let you know about that little matter we discussed. Okay?"

Liam tried to summon up a responding smile. "Or you could just have Jacob call me directly."

Allie looked puzzled...as well she should. "Okay. I'll see what he wants to do. But he might not want to risk getting Mary on the line."

Liam hadn't thought of that. "Then I guess you'd better make the call."

She brightened. "Okay. Good night, Liam."

"Good night, Allie."

Liam was out the door. *Hell, what a mess,* he thought as he walked toward the Jeep. But he was the one who'd made the mess because he couldn't keep his hands and lips off Allie. He would just have to make sure that he was never alone with her in the future.

Chapter Seven

Over the next two weeks, Liam managed to pretty much avoid seeing Allie. He intended to visit Jake on a regular basis, however, to establish a relationship with him, which would help in his adoption suit. But even without this inducement, he would have had a hard time staying away from the little guy. Consequently, while avoiding Allie but needing to see Jake, he was a frequent visitor at Kayla's, dropping in for an hour or so nearly every day.

Once, though, Allie showed up while he was leaving. She must have seen his car out front, but he was taken completely by surprise when they met at the door.

"Allie— Hello." She looked so radiant standing in the early October sunshine. Her hair gleamed golden and her skin glowed.

"Hello, Liam." Her manner was reticent. "How are you?"

"I'm fine. And you?" The strained politeness between them was inevitable, considering they'd separated two weeks ago after a passionate embrace in her kitchen, followed by complete silence and avoidance on his part.

"I'm fine, too," she answered. She smiled tentatively.

"I'm…er…glad you're fine." *Hell, how lame was that?*

They stood there for another awkward moment, then she said, "Well, I guess I'd better go in. I have to go back to the house and see a couple more patients before I'm actually done for the day." Then she looked at him…really looked at him instead of darting him another quick, embarrassed glance between their stilted exchanges. "It's good to see you."

Her tone was warm, the look in her eyes questioning, wounded, hopeful. He wanted to say, *It's good to see you, too…more than you'll ever know.* But that was out of the question.

He forced a smile. "I'll let you go. Have a nice evening." Then, to avoid seeing the reaction to his cool farewell, he turned quickly and headed for his car.

The next day, he sat in Kayla's living room on a sofa by a sunny window, feeding Jake a bottle and looking out at the orange and gold trees and bright red sumac bushes. Kayla was in the other room, trying to put Travis down for a nap. "Try" was the operative word, because Travis fought sleep like a tiger. Then, once he finally succumbed, he slept like the dead.

As Jake drifted to sleep, Liam's thoughts drifted to the subject that consumed most of his waking—and some of his sleeping—hours. He thought of Allie and their intertwined and complicated lives. Seeing her and hearing her voice the day before had brought back all the feelings of that night in her kitchen and the kisses they'd shared. He ached to hold her again. But he was determined not to let a transitory attraction make the future even more difficult for both of them.

Liam's lawyer, a Mr. Conrad Lewis, had looked carefully into international adoption laws, as well as Utah state laws, and had prepared a good case. According to Utah law, abandoned babies could not be adopted till they were six months old, but adoption proceedings could be *started* any time before then.

Mr. Lewis had initially thought it reasonable to wait till Sheriff Renshaw's investigation had died down a bit, but Doug was a stubborn and angry man and he continued to follow up on even the flimsiest of tips to try to find Jake's mother.

Doug had even put on display in his office the little quilt Jake had been wrapped in when Liam found him. He kept hoping someone would recognize the fabric in some of the patches. In Mr. Lewis' stated opinion, if they waited for Doug to give up and close the case, they might be waiting for Hell to freeze over.

Then, when Liam found out from Kayla that Allie hadn't yet filled out the basic forms required for adoption, Mr. Lewis saw it as an opportunity for them to beat her to the punch, so to speak. Apparently, since she was the foster mother and she had friends in Social Services, Allie considered her adoption of Jake as a sure thing. Liam filing papers first would probably play favorably with a judge. That is, if the judge wasn't another of Allie's friends or maybe even a relative!

Mr. Lewis told Liam that the minute he was ready to ''go public'' about his intentions to adopt Jake, he would start the process. He urged Liam to act before Allie had a chance to. Naturally Liam had mixed emotions. He loved Jake more and more as the days passed and wanted him in his life permanently, but revealing his intentions to everyone would open up a big bag of worms. And everyone would label him the biggest worm in the bag!

Liam's main concern with revealing his intentions was the repercussions it might have on Bea. Bea was improving. She'd met with Dr. Jacob Lockwood several times over the past two weeks, and the man was working wonders with her! She was eating better, sleeping better, generally behaving more like a five-year-old girl *should* behave. Liam was full of hope again.

But once Jacob knew that Liam was trying to take his namesake, Jake, away from his granddaughter, he'd probably waste no time at all in ending his sessions with Bea.

To make things more complicated, Allie was the one who recommended her grandfather and initially set up the appointments. Liam owed Allie for Bea's improved health. How would Allie feel when she found out he had filed for adoption of Jake? That he had been underhanded and had misrepresented himself—not by out-and-out lying, but by saying nothing? She would feel betrayed, of course. Betrayed and used. And she'd be right.

Liam *couldn't* give up Jake. That was impossible.

Having Jake in his life had made him feel alive again. But how could he be so cruel to Allie?

Liam shook off his grim mood and smiled when a frazzled-looking Kayla came back into the room. "Did he finally go to sleep?"

Kayla collapsed in a chair across from the sofa and gave a rueful smile. "Do you hear any hollering?"

Liam chuckled. "No."

"That means he's asleep." Kayla sighed and shook her head. "I'm glad Jake's such a good baby. Poor Travis has been like this since he was born. We thought it was colic at first, but when his hyperactivity and sleep problems continued, I could no longer fall back on that explanation."

"Have you had him tested for allergies or… er…behavioral problems?" Liam had spent a lot of time with Kayla and Travis and he was sincerely interested in the welfare of both, but he wasn't sure how nosy he ought to be.

"Only on a limited basis," Kayla admitted. She apparently saw his concerned look and added with a note of impatience in her voice, "Limited because I have a limited *income,* Liam. I can't afford all those tests. And I wouldn't be able to afford the medications they'd probably prescribe like so much penny candy."

"Insurance?" Liam ventured.

"My ex-husband is a deadbeat who moves from job to job, and we're lucky if we get child support. Insurance is a luxury I haven't enjoyed for some time."

"But I'm sure Allie would—"

"I try not to take money from Allie except when I'm desperate," Kayla interrupted, sitting forward in her chair and speaking forcefully. "And I *do* get desperate now and then. I'm certainly not going to let her foot the bill for a bunch of tests that probably won't show anything, anyway. Travis is just an active kid."

Liam wasn't going to argue with her. After all, she could be right. "How do you get your rest, Kayla? You take care of Jake and Travis all day, usually without a break. And I suppose Travis doesn't sleep any better at night?"

Kayla sat back in her chair. "No such luck." She smiled. "But I have a trick. I take him for rides at night when he can't settle down. Sometimes I'm cruising the streets of Annabella at three o'clock in the morning."

"You have a car? I've never seen it."

"It's in the garage. I rarely take it out during the day. To save on gas, I usually walk most places, like to the store or the park, or Allie's place. That way I have gas for my night drives."

"Is it safe?" Liam wasn't sure it was such a good idea for a young, single mother to be in the habit of driving her child around town in the wee hours of the morning. He doubted she had a cell phone to use in case of emergencies.

"Oh, this town's dead at night. You ought to know *that* by now. Sometimes I see Doug driving around, too, making the rounds, making sure 'all's right with the world' in little old Annabella." Her pretty, round face suddenly drooped into a sulk. "If I wave, he'll wave back, but he never stops to talk. I suppose if I was in trouble, he'd stop, 'cause he's the sheriff. But if I was *Allie,* he'd stop just to shoot the breeze. Heck, he'd stop just to sit and look at her. But I'm not Allie.''

Liam had seen plenty of evidence that Kayla was envious—no, downright jealous—of her older sister. Now he was wondering if Kayla had the hots for her ex-brother-in-law. Or maybe she only wanted something Allie had—although what Allie had in this case was an ex-spouse who was too stubborn or stupid to give up on her. But, in a way, he couldn't blame Doug for trying. Allie was a prize.

But none of this mattered, Liam told himself. He determinedly turned his thoughts to the original subject of his conversation with Kayla. Travis and money. He was just considering the idea of offering Kayla a loan—maybe she'd accept help if it wasn't from her sister—when he glanced out of the window and saw Jacob Lockwood and Bea walking down the street toward the house.

Liam had dropped off Bea at the downtown drugstore over an hour ago where she and her friend, ''Dr. Jake,'' were going to have a root-beer float and just chat. Liam was supposed to pick her up in twenty minutes at the same spot, but apparently he'd been saved the trip.

Liam didn't think Bea had the slightest idea that Dr. Jake was actually acting as her doctor, that their outings were therapeutic. If the weather was good they went to the park, or walked around town. If the weather was bad, they had hot chocolate at Bill and Nada's Diner, or went to the library and sat at a table by a window and talked quietly while it rained outside. They were never in an office environment because that might trigger her anxiety or reservations about talking to her new friend.

Yes, Bea had taken to Dr. Jake from their first meeting and had seemed to think of him as her friend ever since. She looked forward to their outings and never questioned why or how their friendship came about. Maybe she enjoyed the outings so much, she didn't dare wonder why he was suddenly such a big part of her life.

"Here comes your grandfather and Bea," Liam announced.

"Oh, good! More company. I *love* company." Kayla shook off her sulks and jumped up to answer the door. "Gramps! How's it going? Hi, Bea. Come on in. Your daddy's here."

Bea hurried in ahead of Jacob with a big smile on her face. Her cheeks were pink from the autumn nip in the air. "Hi, Daddy!" When she saw the baby asleep in his lap, she put her index finger in front of her mouth and whispered, "I didn't know baby Jake was taking a nap. I'll shush."

"Don't worry, Bea," Kayla told her. "Jake's around Travis all day. He's used to noise and nothing much wakes up either of them when they're really out."

"That's where they get the expression 'sleeping like a baby,' Bea," Jacob said. He kissed Kayla and gave her a hug, then stood in the middle of the room with his hands in his trouser pockets, rocking back and forth on his heels. He fixed his penetrating gaze on Liam. "Hello, Liam. I thought we might find you here."

Liam immediately felt defensive, but he tried not to show it. Although Liam saw Jacob every time he dropped off or picked up Bea, the two of them never really talked. Jacob had made it clear from the beginning of his sessions with Bea that he did not want a lot of information or theorizing from Liam about what was wrong with his daughter. He knew the basic facts about Bea's recent health and behavior, and that her mother had died a year ago, and that was enough. He felt that extra talk with the parent might prejudice him to think one way or the other, so to avoid that, he drew conclusions solely from his conversations with the child.

"Well, you were right," Liam finally said with a polite smile. "And now that you've found me, was there something you wanted to talk to me about?"

Jacob turned to Kayla. "Kayla, honey, have you got some milk and cookies in the kitchen? Bea and I got mighty hungry walking home from the drugstore."

Kayla's eyes narrowed speculatively as she looked from Liam to her grandfather and back. "Sure, Gramps."

There was a long pause, then Jacob gave Kayla a pointed look. She understood, but wasn't happy about it. "I suppose you want me and Bea to go get the milk and cookies. And take our time, right?" she added with a petulant pout.

Jacob pretended to ignore Kayla's attitude and nodded. "Would you? I'd be grateful." Then he looked down at Bea, his dark eyes crinkling up in the corners as he smiled warmly at her. "You don't mind helping, do you, Bea?"

Bea smiled back, eager to help. "I don't mind, Dr. Jake. But I'm not very hungry. We just had a root-beer float, remember?"

Jacob chuckled and patted her gently on the head. "Yes, I remember. But I guess it just wasn't enough for me."

Kayla continued to look suspicious and annoyed about being left out of the conversation, but ushered Bea out of the room and into the kitchen at the back of the house anyway. Liam was sure that Jacob wanted to talk to him about Bea and was amazed that Kayla didn't understand and was behaving so immaturely. But since it wasn't the first time he'd noted that personality trait in her, he really shouldn't continue to be surprised.

He turned to Jacob. "So, now that we're alone, you can speak freely about Bea."

Jacob shook his head. "I'm not ready to talk to you about Bea."

For a sick moment, Liam was afraid Jacob had figured out his plans to adopt Jake. He'd known he'd be at Kayla's, didn't he? "Er…then what *do* you want to talk about?"

"Today, and not for the first time, your daughter suggested that we invite Mary to join us on one of our little excursions."

This took Liam completely off-guard. He continued to lock gazes with the old man, but didn't have the slightest idea what he was thinking. "Why do you think she did that?"

Jacob crossed his arms and slanted his head to the side. "Why? Well, I suppose because she loves her grandmother. Bea's been enjoying our treks around town, but it makes her feel bad about her Gran stayin' cooped up all the time.''

Liam continued to examine Jacob's face. ''Are you sure this was *Bea's* idea, Jacob?''

Jacob's face and voice remained expressionless. ''Absolutely.''

Liam sighed and adjusted Jake slightly in his arms. *Oh God, I think I see another complication developing.* ''So what are you thinking? That this would be a good idea?''

''I'm thinking that if it's important enough for Bea to bring it up every time we get together, maybe we should give it a try. It might do her some good.''

Liam raised his brows. ''It might do good for whom, Jacob? Bea or Mary? Or maybe…you?''

Jacob finally let a little expression creep into his face. He smiled wistfully. ''All of us, I reckon.''

''Okay,'' Liam said carefully. ''And who do you think should do the inviting? You, me or Bea?''

''I think it should be me. And I think it should be soon. Do you think—'' Jacob stopped himself and chuckled. ''I was going to ask you if you thought she'd be home right now. Of course she's home.''

He walked over and picked up the phone. Liam watched, incredulous. When he made up his mind to do something, apparently it took no time at all for Jacob Lockwood to act on his decision.

''Hello, Mary?'' Jacob turned away, probably to hide the myriad emotions that were showing up on his face as he talked to his first love a half-century after they'd last seen each other. ''It's Jacob.''

Now Liam was imagining his grandmother, on the other end of the line, pressing her hand to her chest, a look of astonishment on her face.

Liam decided to give Jacob some privacy and left the room. He tiptoed quietly into Kayla's room where she kept Travis's old crib and laid the baby inside, carefully covering him up with the blanket. He gave Jake one last look, then headed for the kitchen, where he found Kayla and Bea sitting at the table with an open package of Oreos and a half-gallon of milk between them.

Bea had propped her chin in her hands and appeared to be watching Kayla eat. She turned when Liam appeared at the door and said, "I'm really not hungry, Daddy. Is that okay?"

"Oh! Liam!" Kayla jumped up guiltily. "We were going to bring the cookies to you, but I thought I'd give you and Gramps a little more time to talk. And Bea says she just ate, so—"

"That's right, she did. Now please just sit back down and finish your snack, Kayla. You deserve it after chasing Travis around all day."

Kayla blushed. "Boy, my ex-husband didn't think so. I never felt comfortable eating in front of him."

Liam thought that was probably why Kayla ate when her husband *wasn't* around and consequently put on a little too much weight. From their conversations, and without Kayla dwelling on the subject, Liam had concluded that her ex-husband, Brad, had been a complete jerk.

Liam sat down. "Eating is even better with company. Pass the cookies, please."

Kayla beamed and sat down, too. "Want some milk?"

Liam smiled. "Of course."

Kayla was pouring Liam a big glass of foamy two-percent when Jacob appeared at the doorway. "Just one more private word with you, Liam?"

Kayla frowned and set down the milk carton with a thud. Liam pretended not to notice and followed Jacob back into the living room. He peered closely at the old man to see if he could tell how the phone call went by the expression on his face. He couldn't. "Well, what did she say, Jacob?"

"She said she thought we ought to meet first, just the two of us, so Bea doesn't have to witness our first awkward meeting after fifty years apart." He gave a quick, satisfied nod. "Smart woman, your grandmother. Always was."

"So…?"

Now Liam could see something like happiness in the gleam of Jacob's dark eyes and in the slight puffing of his chest—kind of like a bird about to do a mating dance. "I'm picking her up tonight and we're having dinner at Rosie's Italian Restaurant."

Liam couldn't help but be happy for Jacob, and for his grandmother. It was about time the two of them made up and became friends again. Yes, it would cause even more complications in the "baby scheme" of things, but he'd deal with that when the time came.

Now it was Jacob's turn to prompt Liam with, "So? Are you okay with this, young man?"

"Absolutely. And even if I wasn't okay with it, I wouldn't stand in Gran's way." Liam gave Jacob a rueful look. "And I don't think any objections on my part would stand in *your* way, either."

Jacob grinned. "I think we're beginning to understand each other."

Liam was afraid of that. The last thing he wanted was for Jacob to completely understand him.

ALLIE WAS HAVING a horrible day. She'd been up most of the night with a headache and, perhaps sensing her restlessness, Jake woke up three times, crying, and had a hard time going back to sleep. Allie was exhausted even before she left the house that morning.

To make matters worse, an early-season flu was going around town and several extra patients had shown up at the office for fit-me-in appointments. It was after six by the time she was able to pick up Jake from Kayla's, and Kayla was in a rotten mood. She was complaining about Gramps keeping a secret from her and sending her out of the room so he could talk to Liam McAllister privately. Imagine, she'd sulked, being treated like a child in her own house!

Allie was dying of curiosity and was tempted to ask for details, but she didn't dare get Kayla started or she might be there for an hour listening to her sister's long list of grievances. Allie loved Kayla dearly and empathized with all the challenges she had in her life, and even though Kayla never took her advice, Allie knew it probably did her good just to vent. But tonight Allie was too tired and too hungry to accommodate Kayla, and Jake was fussing, too, obviously hungry for his bottle. She just wanted to get home and settle in for the night.

Besides, the last person Allie wanted to hear about and talk about was Liam McAllister. She did *not* understand that man! Or maybe she did understand him and didn't want to. Obviously he regretted those incredible kisses they'd shared in her kitchen two weeks ago. At least *she'd* thought they were incredible....

Allie loaded Jake in the car and headed home, thoughts of Liam McAllister still gnawing away at her peace of mind and making her head throb, again. She had talked with him the day after their steamy kitchen encounter, but just to set a time and place for Bea's first meeting with Gramps. He'd been nice, grateful, polite, but...cool. She'd decided he was just feeling a little bewildered by what had happened between them—she was feeling the same—then waited for him to call and invite himself over for dinner again. Surely he wouldn't be able to resist both Jake and her as one enticing package. After all, those kisses were *so*... Well, at least *she'd* thought so.

When three, then four days passed, Allie was toying with the idea of calling *him* and inviting him over, or asking about Bea's sessions with Gramps. But she resisted, and after awhile she began to chide herself for thinking that Liam McAllister had ever been romantically interested in her at all.

A real low point came when, shopping at Safeway one day, she saw a small head shot of Liam squeezed into a corner on the front page of the *Global Intruder*. His eyes were sunken and deeply shadowed underneath, his beard at least four days old. He looked miserable. The small caption read, Lonely Lord,

Mourning His Lost Love, Leaves London, details on page 35.

Allie grabbed the tabloid with a sequined, over-weight Elvis on the cover at the last minute and, shamefaced, pushed it toward Luanne Merryweather, Safeway's head checkout cashier for the last twenty-five years. Luanne was a mother of three grown-up girls Allie's age, easygoing and talkative. She knew a lot about the people of Annabella just by the items they purchased, and Allie's life had been chronicled in the same way.

Luanne was cashier when a young Allie bought candy, comics, Clearasil, teen magazines and her first supply of Kotex. She knew when Allie switched to tampons, *Cosmopolitan* and thick historical romance novels. She didn't blink an eye when Allie bought her first condoms and, later, a succession of pregnancy tests when she and Doug were trying to have a baby. But for some reason, Allie's purchase of the tabloid was too much for Luanne to resist commenting on.

"Reading up on 'im, I see." She winked and Allie blushed crimson.

"I don't know what you mean, Luanne."

Luanne looked smug. "Sure you do, sweetie. I'm surprised there's a copy left. The *Global Intruder*'s been selling like hotcakes today. And I don't think it's because some teenager in Oklahoma saw Elvis at a Chuckarama last Sunday."

Allie knew it was useless to argue. Besides, if everyone else in Annabella was reading about Liam, that removed any suspicion that she might actually have some *extra* interest in the man.

Later Allie read the article and found out that Liam was thought to be on a remote, exclusive island in the Caribbean. She almost laughed at how wrong they were! But then she sobered as she read on and the person writing the piece listed all the possible women who might win Liam's heart and restore his happiness. Allie's eyes widened as she read the list. She recognized most of the names, which included European aristocracy, famous models, rock divas and movie stars.

She put down the paper and laughed. She laughed until she cried. Then she cried just to cry. It didn't last long. She didn't allow it to. It was ridiculous to get involved with a man like Liam McAllister, anyway. Wasn't that what she'd been telling herself all along? But it didn't stop the yearning, dammit.

That was nearly a week ago and now Allie had regained her perspective. Well, she'd nearly lost it again when she saw him at Kayla's yesterday, but it was back. Right now all she wanted was home and dinner, a couple of aspirin, and Jake—

Uh-oh. She just remembered that there was nothing in the fridge but steak sauce and celery. She had planned to go shopping tonight, but it was too late and she was too tired. Besides, it was past time for Jake's bottle and his nightly lullaby in Grandma Lockwood's rocking chair.

She was just coming up to Rosie's Italian Restaurant on the left and impulsively decided to go in and buy some takeout chicken lasagna and Caesar salad. It was Friday night and they got lots of calls for delivered food on the weekends, so this would probably be a quicker way to get her order.

Allie parked the car directly in the front of the restaurant, on a slight slope, where a car had luckily just pulled out. She looked in the back seat and saw that Jake had dozed off. The car was warm and the motor had lulled him to sleep. If she took him out, he'd start fussing again, and she was only going to be inside for maybe three minutes. Rosie always had plenty of chicken lasagna made up and individual salads in take-out containers ready to go for drop-ins like herself.

Allie sat there for a moment, debating. She knew you weren't supposed to leave babies alone in vehicles. But it wasn't hot outside, so Jake wouldn't be in danger of heatstroke. And she wouldn't leave the keys in the car and the motor running, which was an open invitation to kidnappers and car thieves. She smiled at the ludicrous idea of there being any kidnappers or car thieves in Annabella in the first place. She'd only be inside for a couple of minutes....

Allie turned off the ignition, pushed the button that locked all the doors at once, shoved her keys in the pocket of her jacket, got out and shut the door behind her as quietly as possible. Peering through the window, she could see that Jake was still fast asleep, so she hurried into Rosie's and went straight to the counter. Fortunately there were no other customers before her.

She told Sally, the young woman who was simultaneously running the cash register and the takeout counter, what she wanted. Sally went into the kitchen to get her order and, although she was sure no one would steal it and its precious cargo, Allie moved to stand by the steamed-up front window where she could keep an eye on her car. While turning toward the window, however, she happened to glance past the takeout counter at the diners in the restaurant.

Allie quickly recognized almost everyone there, but then she saw something that made her feel like one of those cartoon characters with their eyes popping out of their heads, coiled springs the only thing keeping the goggling eyeballs attached to their sockets! At a table in a cozy corner of the restaurant, Allie saw her grandfather sitting with...Mary McAllister!

Gramps was wearing his best teal-blue sweater, the one that complemented his gray hair and made his brown eyes look darker and more expressive than ever. He had on a tie, too. Not a string tie, either, but a regular go-to-Salt Lake kind of tie. Obviously this meeting was important to him.

Mary was wearing a neat little melon-colored suit, tailored to fit her dainty figure perfectly. But most no-ticeable about the looks of both Mary and Gramps were their smiles and the animated way they were talk-ing to each other.

Allie's first reaction to seeing the two of them to-gether was surprise. The second was a visceral pang of envy. How wonderful that they'd managed to come to terms with their past and all the years that had sep-arated them, and now seemed to be thoroughly enjoy-ing each other's company! But oh how much Allie wished for a similar kind of relationship!

Suddenly Sally was back with her order and Allie quickly collected herself and moved back to the counter, only to be discomposed in the next moment when she realized she'd left her purse in the car!

Allie was embarrassed. She was so scatterbrained today! "I'm sorry, Sally. I left my purse in the car. I'll be back in a jiff. I'm parked just out front—"

But when Allie turned and motioned toward where her car was parked, it wasn't there! With her heart in her throat, she ran to the window, swiped away the steam with her hand, and stared out. Her car had rolled down the slight incline of the parking space and ended up clear across the street! Its rear tires were sitting in the ditch in front of Orin Gable's house, its dead headlights tilted up and staring at her accusingly.

"My baby!" she cried out.

Chapter Eight

Half the restaurant must have heard Allie's frightened exclamation. By the time she ran out of the place, crossed the street, unlocked the car door with shaking hands, unbuckled a crying Jake and lifted him into her arms, a dozen people were standing around.

"He's not hurt, Allie. Just got woke up with a little jolt, that's all. Calm down, hon. It's all right."

Through a haze of fear, Allie finally registered that her grandfather was beside her, one hand resting comfortingly on her shoulder. She'd buried her face in Jake's sweet-smelling hair and when she looked up and felt the cool evening air on her damp cheeks, she realized she'd been crying.

"Gramps, I must not have put the car in parking gear," she confided miserably. "How could I have left him in the car? I knew I shouldn't. I—"

"Don't fret about it, Allie," Gramps soothed. "No harm came to him."

"But something *could* have happened to him! A car could have come along and rammed right into—"

"But it didn't." Now Gramps' voice was less consoling and had taken on a no-nonsense tone. "Pull yourself together, Allie. I'll have someone drive you and Jake home, then arrange to have your car towed out of the ditch and brought to the house. Right now Jake needs you to be calm. It's the only way he'll settle down. Now, take a couple of deep breaths.''

Gramps was right. Allie needed to calm down. As she closed her eyes and took the deep breaths her grandfather recommended, she heard the murmuring crowd dispersing. Gramps and Mary were shooing them gently away. In addition to her own painful recognition of having used extremely poor judgment and been uncharacteristically careless, Allie was aware that the murmurings coming from the crowd weren't all sympathetic. She was sure she'd heard the word *irresponsible* more than once.

Now Allie was filled with doubt. Not just because other people were questioning her ability to care for a baby, but because *she* was. Kayla was right. When you were the sole support for a child—financially, physically, emotionally—and there was no one to help out when you were tired or sick, single parenthood was hard.

Allie's eyes filled with tears again, but she forced them back and bounced Jake gently on her shoulder, rubbing his back and softly singing her grandmother's little ditty. *Hi-dumma, do-dumma, hi-dumma-diddle-dumma.* Soon Jake quieted and rested his head against her chest.

''Dr. Lockwood?''

Allie turned and saw Joseph Martinelli, Rosie's husband, walking toward her. ''I told your grandfather I would drive you home.''

"Oh, okay. Where is Gramps?"

"He's inside, calling someone to tow your car. He said he'd check with you first thing in the morning. Are you ready?"

Allie smiled weakly. "Yes, Joseph. More than ready. Just let me get Jake's diaper bag."

"I'll get it," Joseph offered. "You just hold on to that baby, okay?"

Joseph was trying to be kind, but his words just made Allie feel even more guilty. She should have been holding on to Jake when she'd gone into the restaurant. Her mind kept returning to thoughts of what might have happened.

"You'd better take this, too," Joseph said, handing Allie her purse.

Allie felt her face grow hot with chagrin. She'd been about to leave her purse in the car again!

Joseph stayed quiet as he drove her home in his minivan, which smelled aromatically of the spices and tomato products he regularly transported. Allie was grateful for his restraint and thanked him warmly when he dropped her off at the house.

Once inside, Allie wasted no time in grabbing a bottle for Jake and rocking him to sleep. She didn't even take the time to remove her jacket or swallow some aspirin for her pounding headache. As he drifted off to sleep, she sat and stared at him, love and anguish squeezing her heart like a vise.

She'd been sitting that way for nearly an hour, when the doorbell rang. She startled, then remembered that someone was supposed to be towing her car home and that was probably them. They'd need to be paid. She

looked around for her purse, cursed under her breath
when she discovered that once again she couldn't locate the damn thing, then walked to the door with Jake
still in her arms.

"I'm sorry, but can you wait a minute while I put
him down in his—" Allie had started speaking before
the door was even open. When she saw Liam standing
on her threshold instead of a tow-truck driver, the remaining words stuck in her throat. He wore a dark
gray trench coat over a black turtleneck sweater and
jeans. He looked tense and troubled.

"Sure, I'll wait," he said, then walked into the
house and shut the door behind him.

Damning the fates that were making this entire day
and night an unending nightmare, Allie left the room
and put Jake in his crib. She dreaded going back into
the living room and facing Liam. He must have heard
about the accident. *Which was all her fault.* She could
only imagine what he was going to say to her. By
showing up now after avoiding her for two weeks, he
must have some pretty strong feelings to express.

Wiping her damp hands against her thighs, she
walked slowly into the living room. He was still standing by the door, looking stern.

"I guess you heard," she said.

He nodded.

"Bad news travels fast. I'm sorry I broke up your
grandmother's date with Gramps. She probably
couldn't wait to tell you what an idiot I was."

Allie wanted to bite her tongue. It was only natural
that Mary would tell Liam what happened, and it had
probably been done with no malicious intent at all.

Liam stepped forward. "To begin with, you don't have to apologize for breaking up Gran's date with Jacob. They're still at Rosie's, as far as I know."

"Oh," was all Allie could manage.

"And it was Jacob who told me what happened, not Mary."

Allie frowned. "But why—?"

Liam took a couple steps closer. "Because he asked me to tow your car out of the ditch."

Allie's eyes widened. "But why—?"

Liam shrugged. "Because I was available and the Jeep's great for towing, I guess. Does it bother you that he called me?"

Allie felt her face heating up again. "I just don't know why he called *you*. I mean, it doesn't *bother* me."

But it did bother her. It bothered her a lot. In such a small town, he was bound to hear about it eventually, but why tonight? She needed time to process what happened and recover from it. She was so ashamed. From that first night, Liam had doubted her abilities to take care of Jake. Now she'd proved him right.

"Allie? Hey, look at me." Liam was standing right in front of her now, so close she could smell the cold night air on his trench coat.

Allie realized she'd been staring at the floor, and tears were once again building up. She looked at Liam, but instead of the condemnation she was afraid she'd see in his eyes, she saw something else. Compassion. Empathy.

It was too much. She'd have fought off the torrent of emotions if he'd criticized her, lectured her. But his kindness was the last straw. Bursting into tears, Allie fell into Liam's arms.

Allie wasn't sure how long she cried, but Liam held her the whole time. He rubbed her back and whispered soothing words into her hair. It felt so good being held and comforted…especially by Liam. He was good at it. And his chest was so warm and hard and nice to cuddle against. His hands felt so good against her back.…

When Allie realized her thoughts were taking on a sensual tone, she grew embarrassed and pulled away. How could she let her attraction to Liam distract her from her own well-deserved guilt feelings?

"You're very kind," she mumbled as she wiped her eyes with the back of her hand. "When I know you're thinking what an idiot I am. How irresponsible I was for leaving Jake in the car. What if—?"

"Allie, when was the last time you ate?" Liam interrupted. "And why haven't you taken off your jacket yet?"

Allie stared at him, confused. "Don't you want me to talk about what happened?"

He took her by the shoulders and gave a short, exasperated sigh. "Sure, if that's what you want. But first you need to get more comfortable, Allie. You've probably got one hell of a headache from all that crying."

"I *do* have a headache," she admitted, "but I've had one all day."

His hands squeezed her shoulders. "So, you need to do something about that, right? Why don't you start by taking off your jacket and shoes and washing your face? Better yet, why don't you take a bath? In the meantime, I'll cook something for you to eat.''

Allie continued to stare at him, bewildered and bewitched by his kindness, unwillingly warmed by his touch. ''Unless you're a marvel with celery and steak sauce, there's nothing in the house to eat.''

''Then I'll order something from Rosie's. That's why you were there, isn't it?''

''Yes, but—''

''What did you order?''

''Chicken lasagna and Caesar salad, but—''

''Okay. That sounds good to me, too. Where do you keep your aspirin? You do have aspirin, don't you?''

Allie gave a crooked smile. ''I'm a doctor. Of course I have aspirin.''

''Along with bottles and bottles of formula and boxes of diapers, I'll wager,'' Liam added.

''I was going to go to the store today to buy groceries, but there's a flu going around and my patient load was—''

Liam stooped a little and peered into her face. ''In other words, you're taking care of Jake's needs and everyone else in town, but not yourself. If you don't take care of yourself, Allie, you won't be any good to anyone else. What happened tonight should make that quite clear.''

Allie opened her mouth to argue, but realized she didn't have a leg to stand on. He was right. Besides it was much more pleasant just standing there and staring into those beautiful green eyes of his.

Liam straightened up and released her shoulders...dang it. ''But I'm doing exactly what I told you not to do, aren't I? Talking about it can wait till you're feeling a little more human. Baths are great for that."

Now he took her arm and led her down the hall till she was standing in front of her bedroom door. She wondered, vaguely, how he knew where her bedroom was.

"You soak, I'll order dinner." Then he gently pushed her inside and closed the door behind her.

Trudging to her dresser, Allie stood in front of the mirror and took off her earrings. Grimacing at her reflection, she decided that Liam was probably hoping a bath would make her look, as well as feel, a little more human. Her face was blotched, her mascara running and her nose as red as Rudolph's.

She took off her jacket, then her blouse and slacks. She was down to her bra and panties when there was a soft knock on her door.

Grabbing her blouse and clutching it to her chest, she called nervously, "Yes? What do you want?"

"Don't sound so alarmed," he answered with a wry note in his voice. "I just wanted to give you these aspirin so they can start working while you have your bath."

Allie went to the door, stood behind it and opened it just far enough to peek around at Liam. He was holding a glass of water and two aspirin, and making a real effort to keep his gaze strictly fixed on her face. She was well hidden behind the door, so she thought his gentlemanly conduct rather sweet.

She smiled. "Make that a glass of wine and three aspirin and I think I might have a fighting chance against this particular headache."

He raised his brows. "That bad, huh? Well, you're the doctor. Be right back."

She waited at the door, not daring to move or take off any more items of clothing till he returned...even though she had plenty of time to finish undressing and put on her robe. She marvelled that her horrible day was ending with a drop-dead gorgeous Viscount taking care of her. Then she remembered *why* he was taking care of her and frowned. She didn't deserve to be happy!

Liam brought back the chilled wine and aspirin which she took without meeting his eyes, mumbled a humble "thank-you," then quickly closed the door.

Despite her desire to stay angry with herself and be miserable, the bath, the wine and the aspirin gradually did their jobs. Her muscles relaxed, her headache disappeared, and she definitely felt more human when she left her bedroom half an hour later.

She trusted she *looked* more human, too, despite the fact that she'd only allowed herself to put on a cozy, schlumpy pair of sweatpants, one of her oversize flannel shirts, and fuzzy bedroom slippers. She wasn't going to fool herself into thinking Liam was the slightest bit interested in her appearance, so why dress up? Besides, primping might give him the wrong impression...or the *right* one, depending on how you looked at it.

She couldn't face him without makeup, though, and a little splash of perfume. She *did* have her pride, after all.

Before Allie went to the kitchen, she checked on Jake. He was still sleeping peacefully. She tucked his blanket around his shoulders, kissed the tip of her index finger and pressed it lightly against his plump cheek. Then she turned, took a deep breath and headed down the hall.

The kitchen was filled with the aroma of Rosie's chicken lasagna, Caesar salad and crusty Italian bread. Liam was standing by the sink and turned when he heard the muted thump of Allie's rubber soles on the oak floor. He'd taken off his trench coat and he looked too sexy for words in the torso-skimming black turtleneck he wore.

His eyes took quick stock of her, then he smiled. "Ah, that's better. You look much more comfortable now."

Warmed by his approval, Allie smiled back. Suddenly she realized she was famished.

LIAM HAD NEVER SEEN anyone look better in flannel than Allie. She exuded wholesome, sexy, girl-next-door touchability. And apparently the bath had done wonders to restore her state of mind. It was distressing to see her so upset before.

When Jacob first called him with the news and asked him to tow Allie's car out of the ditch, he'd been livid with anger. What had she been thinking, leaving a baby in a car? And not just any baby, but *Jake*. The child she thought she should be entrusted with to raise and care for.

Liam hadn't questioned Jacob's reasons for calling him instead of a tow service or someone closer to the family, he'd just thrown on his trench coat and grabbed his keys. Bea was busy making Halloween cookies with Mrs. Preedy in the kitchen and he called a quick goodbye as he left the house, promising to be back to tuck her in.

Outwardly he kept his temper as he hooked up Allie's car and towed it home, but inside he was seething. He was feeling much less guilty about his plans to adopt Jake, and he was going to call his lawyer in the morning and tell him to start proceedings. He was ready to go public! And, if push came to shove in a court of law, they could even use Allie's mistake in leaving Jake in the car against her.

But that was before Allie answered the door with Jake in her arms, looking anguished and exhausted and forlorn. She hadn't even taken off her jacket. She was holding Jake like she was afraid to put him down. Her remorse was palpable, and Liam's anger had dissipated like the morning mist under a hot sun.

Hell, everyone made mistakes. He'd made his share....

He had to fight the urge to take her into his arms to comfort her. Then she'd fallen into his arms, sobbing, and he no longer had to fight.

"You're staring at me, Liam."

Liam was embarrassed. Yes, he'd been staring at her since the moment she'd entered the kitchen. "I know. It's just that you look—"

He hesitated. Did he dare tell her he thought she was beautiful? No, that might not be a good idea.

"—so much better."

Allie flashed him a grin that was both shy and rueful. "You could turn a girl's head with compliments like that."

"Sorry, Allie. I'm a little out of practice." *And you're the last person I should be practicing on.*

Liam cleared his throat and became businesslike. "I took the liberty of setting the table. I found everything we need, I think. Plates, silverware, napkins, Parmesan cheese, butter, salt and pepper. And more wine, of course. I had Rosie's send over one of their favorite vintages. You see I *can* find my way around the house and the kitchen, perhaps just as well as your ex-hubby."

Liam hadn't meant for that last part to slip out. Allie might think it pretty pathetic that he'd remembered that comment from the first night they met, but it had rankled him then and, to some degree, it rankled him now. Then it dawned on him that it was entirely possible that he was jealous of Doug Renshaw and was just now realizing it. Did Allie realize it, too?

Liam was grateful that Allie felt no need to comment, but simply sat down at the table and smiled up at him. "This is wonderful. Thank you, Liam."

Liam sat down, too. "Now remember, we aren't going to discuss the er…incident till we're done with dinner. Agreed?"

Allie picked up her wineglass and took a sip. "Agreed. But we can talk about Bea, can't we? And then there's the little matter of your grandmother and my grandfather on a date. A *date,* Liam."

As they worked their way through the delicious meal, they found they shared the same feelings about Jacob and Mary's reunion and apparent reconciliation. They both said they wished they'd been flies on the wall when the two old sweethearts met for the first time after fifty years.

"Well, they looked pretty happy when I saw them at the restaurant," Allie said, as she tore off another piece of Italian bread and spread it with sweet butter. "It was from a distance, but I could swear they were both glowing. And they'd obviously dressed up for each other."

Liam flitted a glance over Allie's flannel shirt and couldn't resist a teasing jab. "Yes, I suppose how one dresses for dinner with the opposite sex reveals the extent to which one wishes to please or entice."

Allie blushed rosy and set down her fork. "Liam, you told me to get *comfortable*. I clean up quite nice for dates, you know."

Liam realized his teasing remark hadn't gone over well at all, and impulsively decided to tell the truth. "Allie, you look enticing in everything I've ever seen you in. If you look even better on dates, no man has a snowball's chance in hell of resisting you."

Allie stared at him, obviously startled by his compliment. Perhaps he'd been too truthful. Perhaps he'd had too much wine.

"How do you think Bea's doing?" she said finally, wisely changing the subject.

"Your grandfather won't talk about it with me—"

"That's his style."

"I know. And that's fine with me. Whatever he's doing with her, whatever they're talking about, I can see the results with my own eyes. She's eating better, sleeping better." He smiled wistfully. "She's turning into my little Busy Bea again. I left her and Mrs. Preedy baking cookies tonight.''

Allie smiled. ''I'm so glad. I'm sure there's nothing more disturbing than worrying over your child's health. Thank God Jake's never been sick yet, but if he was— If anything at all happened to him, I don't know what I'd do.''

Suddenly Allie's eyes filled with tears again. She dabbed at the corners of her eyes with her napkin. ''Sorry, it's still too fresh for me to be unemotional about what happened.''

''It's understandable,'' Liam murmured. ''But while you probably can't quit thinking about what might have happened, you can try to quit blaming yourself. Everyone makes mistakes, and I'm sure you've learned a lesson from this.''

Allie bit her bottom lip, then said thoughtfully, ''That's the closest you've come to lecturing me, Liam, and I must say I'm surprised you haven't been harder on me. You love Jake, too. You probably think you could take better care of him than I do.''

Liam had no answer for that. He'd thought so for a long time. He'd dreamed and planned and plotted to be Jake's parent since the night of his birth. But suddenly he wasn't so sure he'd been thinking straight…or thinking about Jake, for that matter.

Despite what had happened tonight, Allie was a great mother. And he knew she'd get even better as the weeks and years passed. No parent, whether biological or adopting, knew everything there was about raising a child. It was a learn-as-you-go process. Jake would flourish with Allie as his mother. For Jake's sake, Liam couldn't possibly take him away from Allie.

Besides, Liam cared too much for Allie to hurt her in any way. There, he'd admitted it to himself. It wasn't just a sexual attraction. He *cared* for Allie.

"You're not saying anything, Liam," Allie said softly. "Does that mean you agree with me? That you think you—and probably just about anyone else—could take better care of Jake than I can?"

It was such a relief for Liam to be able to believe, and sincerely mean, what he was about to say. He leaned forward and rested his hand on Allie's. "Jake is lucky to have you. You're a wonderful mother to him. Don't ever doubt yourself again."

The gratitude in Allie's misty eyes and tentative smile made Liam's heart swell with pleasure. He was glad he'd come to his senses before revealing his plans to adopt Jake and cause all kinds of problems and heartache. He was glad he'd kept his plans to himself and now Allie and Gran and Jacob need never know.

"I'd better check on Jake," Allie said, breaking the spell.

Liam stood up, too. "And I'd better call Bea and tell her I'm on my way home. I promised to tuck her in."

Allie headed for Jake's bedroom and Liam used the kitchen phone to call home. He was surprised to hear that Gran was still out with Jacob, and Bea had fallen asleep right after her bath.

"Don't fret about it, my lord," Mrs. Preedy said. "Bea fell asleep so quickly, she didn't know who was tucking her in. Even if she remembers in the morning that you said you'd be here, she won't be mad at you, I'm sure.''

"You're probably right, Mrs. Preedy," Liam said. "But I like being there to tuck her in."

"Well, my lord, you've got to have a life of your own to lead, too, now don't you?"

Liam wasn't sure how to reply to this, so he quickly thanked Mrs. Preedy and hung up. He hadn't told her where he was going when he left the house, but did she somehow know?

When Liam got off the phone, Allie still hadn't returned to the kitchen, so he went to the door of Jake's room and looked in. The room was dark except for a night-light by the crib. Allie was standing there, looking down at Jake. Liam hoped she wasn't crying again, blaming herself and feeling guilty. He walked in quietly and stood beside her.

When Allie looked at him, Liam was relieved to see no tears brimming in her eyes or streaming down her cheeks. She looked contented and thoroughly beguiled by…her baby.

"I love to watch him sleep," she whispered.

"I know. It was the same way with Bea."

"Is she waiting up for you?"

"No, she's already asleep."

"Oh, I'm sorry. I kept you away from her, but…but I'm not really sorry. To tell you the truth, I think I needed you even more than Bea tonight."

Liam felt a bittersweet joy blossom in his chest. *She'd needed him. Just like Victoria used to need him.* "I didn't really do anything."

"Yes, you did," she insisted softly. "You were

kind. You tended to me, made me bathe and eat. Fetched me wine and aspirin. Forgave me for being careless, and helped me on the road to forgiving my- self. I must say I'm surprised you've gone to so much trouble. After not seeing you for so long, I thought—''

She didn't continue, but turned away and gazed at Jake again. Liam knew he needed to explain. He took her by the shoulders and gently urged her to look at him. Her expression was uncertain, expectant.

''Allie, after that night when we kissed, I didn't trust myself to spend more time with you. I wasn't sure it was wise for us to get involved that way.''

She trembled, then looked down shyly. ''But you're here now. Does…does that mean you've changed your mind?''

''No. I still think it's probably not wise.'' He felt a sudden tension in her shoulders. In a moment, she'd probably pull away and walk out of the room. He swallowed hard and continued. ''But—''

She waited, then finally looked up. ''But?''

He gave a long, relieved sigh, as if finally giving himself up to fate. He smiled into her big brown eyes and said, ''But right now I don't care. Right now all I can think about is how you smell, how you look, and how you'd feel in my arms.''

She trembled again, but didn't look away. Her lips parted slightly and her eyes glowed with emotion.

His fingers tightened on her shoulders. ''Don't keep me in suspense, Allie. Tell me how you feel. Tell me now if you want me to stay or leave. Because if I stay another minute, I warn you…I won't be wise.''

Allie reached up and wrapped her arms around his neck. ''Oh, Liam… *Stay*.''

Chapter Nine

Allie knew she must be asleep and dreaming. Even in her wildest, wide-awake fantasies, she could never have imagined how wonderful it would feel being carried in Liam's arms to her bedroom. She'd been stunned when he picked her up, and couldn't repress a little cry of surprise. He'd chuckled deep in his throat and advised her, "Don't wake the baby...*please.*"

Allie felt like a precious prize being carted off to Liam's lair. Precious and desirable. Silly her, she'd thought men picked up women and carried them off to the bedroom—or lair—only on soap operas and in miniseries about the rich and famous. Of course, Liam *was* rich and famous. But *she* wasn't, and yet this was really happening!

His arms as they cradled her back and legs were taut and muscled. She could feel his heart beating against her breast. His breath in her hair and against her cheek was warm and smelled sweetly of wine.

As he carried her through the open door of her bedroom, he flipped the light switch that turned on the two lamps on either side of her queen-size bed. He paused just inside the room and looked down at her, a question in his eyes…but there was a persuasive seductiveness, too. She knew what he wanted. He wanted to look at her, see everything. Overcome with shyness, she flipped the lights off. It had been too long since she'd been naked in front of a man. She needed the psychic protection of the dark.

His unspoken question answered, he started toward the bed. But she'd felt the slight, disappointed droop of his wide shoulders.

"No! Wait."

He stopped.

"What, Allie?"

"I…I want the light…*on*."

He hesitated. She could hear him swallow. "Are you sure, darling?"

"Yes." Her tone and her resolve were firm. Besides, she wanted to see *him*, too.

He carried her back to the door, she flipped on the light and they grinned at each other. Then he set her down on her bare feet. Somewhere along the way, she'd kicked off her fuzzy slippers.

"It's been a long time for me, Liam," Allie said.

"For me, too," he admitted. "But something this special is worth waiting for, isn't it?"

She smiled coyly. "How do you know it's going to be special?"

He cupped her face in his beautiful hands and smiled back at her, his green eyes a shadowy, provocative gray in the soft lighting of the bedroom. At that moment the expression "bedroom eyes" took on a whole new meaning for Allie. "I've been haunted day and night by those kisses we shared two long weeks ago. Oh, this is going to be special, all right. Very special, Allie, my love.''

Allie grinned up at him and slid her arms around his narrow waist. "Okay, *my lord*," she teased. "You talk the good talk and your accent is *very* sexy. Now shut up already and start giving me the 'royal treatment.'"

With something like a groan and a laugh, Liam pulled Allie hard against his chest. He bent his head and caught her mouth with his…for the first time all night, for the first time in two long weeks. The kiss was fierce and urgent, and they were both breathless when their lips finally broke contact.

"Allie," he moaned against her cheek, then trailed kisses and nibbles down her throat as he stroked her back and kept her firmly against him.

She loved the feel of him. She loved the way the muscles in his broad shoulders flexed under her questing hands. She loved his strong thighs pressed against hers. Her stomach quivered in response, her nipples hardened and tingled.

They kissed again, this time deeper, lingering. She cupped the back of his head, sifted her fingers through his hair. She wondered, could people die from feeling too much pleasure? Surely *she* was dying. Sinking. Melting. Drowning. Her bones were liquid. If she didn't lie down soon, Liam would have to prop her up against the wall. Although that idea had definite possibilities, too…

"Darling. Let's take this off, shall we?" Liam's hands were on the buttons of her flannel shirt.

Allie opened her eyes and smiled at him through a fog of arousal. "You sound so British."

He raised a brow. "Is that bad?" He was undoing her shirt without even looking at the buttons. One, two, three, and her shirt was starting to gape open.

"Oh no," she assured him, impressed by his agility in the disrobing process. "That's *good*. That's very, very good, *indeed*."

He chuckled. "I think you're making fun of me."

"Not in a million years," she answered on a caught breath. Suddenly her shirt was all the way open and his warm hands were inside, spanning her waist, sliding up her rib cage. Cupping her breasts.

"Pretty bra," he commented, his voice rough. "Who'd have thought such a lacy confection was underneath this flannel shirt."

"I'm glad I wore it," she whispered as her eyes drifted shut and a shiver of desire ran up her spine.

"So you did dress up for me after all," he suggested in a seductive drawl.

"Maybe." She could barely speak. She was weak with wanting him.

"Now let's dress you *down*. And all for me."

Liam slipped the flannel shirt off Allie's shoulders and it fell to the floor. Then he undid her bra and it dropped to the floor, too. She, in turn, helped him pull off his sweater, and finally her hands were on his bare chest. *Heaven.*

For a moment they just stared at each other. "Ah, Allie," he whispered finally. "You're as beautiful as I thought you'd be."

"So are you." Why didn't he touch her? she wondered. If he didn't touch her soon...

Then, mercifully, his hands were on her again. Liam caught Allie by the waist, drew her over to the bed and guided her to sit down. Then he got down on his knees and buried his face between her breasts. Allie took his face in her hands and rested her cheek against his soft hair. The mood was almost reverent, but tense with longing.

Then he was caressing her breasts, kissing them, tugging on the taut nipples with his teeth. Allie's head fell back, drunk with the intense pleasure of it.

Eventually he pulled her to her feet and slipped off her sweatpants and panties. She was completely naked before him. The ardent, admiring look in his eyes made her weak in the knees.

"Liam," she almost pleaded. "I have to lie down. You have to make love to me before I expire on the spot."

He chuckled again, but his voice was shaky. "I'm as ready as you are, darling, believe me. But I just remembered that I don't have a condom with me. Haven't carried one for years. And I don't think you'd want another baby so soon after adopting Jake."

Liam's confession caught Allie off-guard. She was glad he didn't carry a condom in his wallet, as if expecting sex around every corner. But he didn't have a clue that *they* didn't need a condom...at least not to prevent pregnancy. Apparently that bit of her history had not been told to Liam. It surprised her because her infertility—thanks to Kayla and Doug—was common knowledge in Annabella.

But she wasn't going to tell Liam now! Somehow she felt it would diminish her in his eyes. Issues about her infertility had affected her sexuality when she and Doug were married, and she wasn't going to let it ruin this magical night for her!

"I've got condoms. I'm a doctor, after all."

"I was hoping you'd say that."

The condom was acquired and no momentum lost in their headlong tumble into passion. If anything, Allie was even more eager as Liam removed his shoes, socks and…at long last…his jeans and boxers.

Allie was awed by his arousal. She couldn't wait till he was inside her, loving her, making them one.

And soon it was so.

She trembled and ached and arched beneath him. She watched and marvelled as his pleasure matched hers. They made love with an intensity of emotional and physical connection, the likes of which she'd never experienced before. Her climax came first and was sublime, racking her body with wave after wave of pleasure. Then she watched him reach his, and she gloried in her power to please him. Tears welled in her eyes and she wiped them quickly away, afraid for him to see how much he'd moved her.

How much she felt.

How much she loved him.

LIAM WAS JARRED AWAKE by the sound of someone knocking on the front door. He opened his eyes and started to sit up, afraid the noise would rouse the whole house and alarm Bea. Then he realized that he wasn't alone in bed. And he wasn't at Gran's cabin. He was at Allie's.

Allie. Memories of their lovemaking rushed back. And now she was lying next to him, her open palm resting on his chest, her soft breasts pressed against him. They'd fallen asleep in each other's arms. He looked at her peaceful, beautiful face and wished he could wake her up and start the night all over again. But then he looked at the illuminated face of the alarm clock by the bed. It was twelve-thirty in the morning. He needed to get home.

The thumping on the front door started again and he remembered what woke him up in the first place. Allie stirred, moaned, sat up. "What's going on?"

"Someone's at your front door." Liam swung his legs over the side of the bed and picked up his boxers from the floor.

"Must be an emergency," Allie said. "I've got to get dressed. Where's my shirt?"

Still groggy from sleep and wine and lovemaking, they found the clothes they'd discarded in the heat of passion and quickly dressed.

"Do you want me to stay in here till you and your patient are in the examination room? I can leave through the front door while you're busy in the back."

"Whoever's at the door has already seen your car, Liam," Allie said. "They know you're here. Besides, it's only twelve-thirty. A girl's got a right to a social life, doesn't she? Even if she *is* the town doctor."

"I just thought—"

"It's sweet of you to worry about my reputation,

but I don't think it will be immediately obvious that we've been making love."

Liam wasn't so sure about that. They were both disheveled. It definitely didn't look like they'd been playing Scrabble.

She must have seen the doubt on his face. "If you crept out without making an appearance, it would look cheap and shady. I'm not ashamed of anything we've done. Are you?"

"Of course not. I do need to get home, though. I didn't plan on falling asleep. If Bea woke up in the night and wanted me—"

"I understand. You should go. But not like a thief in the night, okay?"

He saw the anxiety in her eyes and nodded. He realized she was more afraid of what a sneaky departure might say about their being together, than how it would appear to whoever was at the door. He had to reassure her. Despite the fact that the knocking on the door continued unabated, Liam caught her by the arms and said, "This *meant* something to me, Allie. There was nothing cheap and shady about it. Okay?"

She gave a weak smile. "Okay. But I guess now's not the time to talk, is it?" She started to leave the room.

"Comb your hair with your fingers," Liam called after her. "It looks like someone couldn't keep their hands out of it."

She grinned. "You'd better do the same."

Suddenly Jake could be heard crying, and Allie groaned.

"I'll tend to Jake," Liam said, right behind her in the hall. "Go ahead and answer the door."

Allie threw a grateful smile over her shoulder and Liam went directly into Jake's room. As he picked up Jake, he heard Allie open the door and then the sound of a man's voice. *Hell,* it was Doug Renshaw.

"Took you long enough to get here," Doug snarled. "Busy?"

"Doug, what are you doing here?" Allie's tone was as frigid and forbidding as an iceberg. "I doubt you're here on official business. Unless there's an emergency, you have no right to—"

Liam heard the door slam shut. "Well, that's where you're wrong. This is official business, and it might even be an emergency. But it looks like I'm too damn late. Did you have a good time, Allie? I hope so, because you're going to regret this night more than you'll ever know."

Liam had heard enough. With a crying Jake held against his shoulder, Liam went down the hall and into the living room. Allie was standing with her arms crossed over her breasts while Doug towered threateningly over her.

"What the hell do you think you're doing?" Liam asked, trying to keep his voice down so he wouldn't frighten Jake. But Jake must have felt the tension because he cried even harder. Allie immediately came forward and took Jake out of Liam's arms.

Doug sneered at Liam. "So you decided to make an appearance, eh, McAllister?"

"Why shouldn't I? I've got nothing to hide."

''That's a good one. From what I hear over in Kamas, you've got plenty to hide.''

Liam's heart skipped a beat, then started again, harder and faster. He told himself to remain outwardly calm. Doug might just be baiting him. ''I have no idea what you're talking about.''

Allie gave a long, fed-up sigh. ''Doug, why are you here? I suppose you saw Liam's car and decided to interfere. When are you going to realize it's over between us?''

''This is not about us, Allie,'' Doug told her in a self-important voice. ''Although I *do* hate to see you make a fool of yourself over this Euro-trash playboy. You don't even know him.''

''I thought I knew *you.* But that didn't stop me from making a fool of myself over you, did it?''

His eyes narrowed. ''I *said*…this is not about us. This is about McAllister and the underhanded crap he's been up to ever since he came to town.''

Liam felt as though he were going to be sick. *Oh God, he knew. He really knew. But why now?*

Allie shifted Jake in her arms, her brows drawn together in a puzzled frown. ''What are you talking about, Doug?''

Doug switched his gaze from Allie to Liam. He smiled unpleasantly. ''It seems his lordship here has been playing us all for fools. He's hired himself—''

''Let me tell her,'' Liam interrupted.

Allie looked surprised, her gaze going back and forth between Liam and Doug. ''Tell me what?''

''Just leave and I'll tell her everything,'' Liam said, still trying to reason with Doug.

Doug shook his head disgustedly. "Why should I do that? And how do I know you'd tell her everything…or anything, for that matter? She's obviously hot for you. She'd probably believe whatever B.S. story you told her. I think I'd better stay and make sure she gets the truth, for once."

"That's pretty ironic coming from you, Doug," Allie threw at him as she bounced Jake in her arms, still trying to calm him. "I don't know what kind of fairy tale you've concocted to make Liam look bad, but I'd appreciate it if you'd just leave. Can't you see this is upsetting Jake? I need to take care of my baby."

"Are you sure he's yours, Allie?" Doug asked her with a fierce look. "Did it ever once cross your mind that someone else might have set their sights on Jake, too?"

Allie froze. "You found the mother? The father? Tell me, Doug. Has someone come forward to claim Jake?"

Liam couldn't stand the terror in Allie's voice. Even if Doug refused to leave, he had to tell Allie the truth and he had to tell her now. This minute. He couldn't stand by while she wondered and worried that she might lose Jake.

"I'm sure that's not what Doug found out in Kamas, Allie," Liam said in a tired voice.

Allie stared at him. "So it *does* have something to do with you?"

"Yes."

She looked at him doubtfully. "Liam, I don't understand."

"I know. I'll explain. But first go get Jake a bottle."

"But—"

"Just do as I say and I promise I'll tell you everything. In the meantime, you've got to calm Jake down."

With one more apprehensive and confused look at him, and then Doug, Allie left to fetch the bottle.

Liam turned to Doug. "You bastard."

"Look who's calling who a bastard," Doug said. "First you try to steal Jake from her, then you sleep with her."

"It's not the way it looks. I was going to tell her tonight."

"Just got side-tracked, eh?"

"Or tomorrow at the latest. I've decided not to file for adoption. I was going to call my lawyer first thing in the morning."

Doug chuckled mirthlessly. "Right. How convenient. You expect me to believe that crap? Well, I don't and Allie won't either. Maybe she enjoyed your little mattress mambo, but she's not stupid."

Liam moved to stand directly in front of Doug. "Look, Renshaw, if you don't quit your trash-talking about Allie—"

"I'm back," Allie announced as she entered the room. "So the two of you'd better quit behaving like a couple of stray dogs in an alley. I want the truth, and I want it now. But speak quietly because I don't want Jake upset anymore than he already is."

Allie sat down on the couch with Jake. She'd put the nipple of the bottle in his mouth and he was drinking hungrily, but his little hands were still waving around like he was agitated.

Liam sat down on the chair across from her, but Doug remained standing. Liam wished with a fervor that Renshaw would make himself scarce, but he didn't blame him for hanging around, either. It was going to be damned hard, though, explaining things to Allie with Doug's angry, jealous presence in the room.

Liam faced Allie, who was looking surprisingly calm, but grim, as if braced for the worst. He gave it to her in a few straightforward sentences. "I hired a lawyer to assist me in adopting Jake. I've kept it a secret from everyone. Even Gran. His name is Conrad Lewis, renowned for his cutthroat abilities in custody issues. He's been looking into all the state and international laws and we've been building a case against you, and for me, as the adopting parent."

Allie was stunned. She couldn't seem to speak for a moment. Her eyes watered up, then she swallowed hard as if pushing back the ache in the back of her throat...the ache that built up just before you cried. Liam waited. Eventually she was able to command herself. "You knew I intended to adopt Jake," she said evenly.

"Yes. But I wasn't going to let that stop me."

She looked as though he'd slapped her. It hurt him to hurt her, but he was determined to be completely honest from then on. Being secretive certainly had not reaped any rewards.

"You knew how much I loved him." Her eyes—those beautiful eyes of hers—were wounded and accusing.

Liam thought about this. "No, not really. Not till

tonight, anyway. I knew you *wanted* him, but so did I.''

"What makes you think you'd have won over Allie, anyway?" Doug interjected. "Did you think your money and your fame would prejudice the authorities in your favor? We don't do things that way around here, McAllister."

Liam ignored Doug and spoke to Allie. "You were so sure you'd get him, with all your connections around here and temporary custody, you haven't even bothered to file adoption papers yet. I was going to beat you to the punch, but I was trying to wait till Bea finished her sessions with your grandfather. As you know, he's helped her tremendously. If I'd gone public about the adoption, I was afraid Jacob would drop Bea out of loyalty to you."

"Loyalty," she repeated dully. "I'm surprised you understand the concept."

Liam winced, but continued. "I knew the fact that you had been caring for Jake all this time would weigh with the authorities, but that's why I took great care to spend as much time with Jake as possible. I love him, of course, and wanted to be with him, anyway. But I had to establish the fact that I had an ongoing relationship with him. That he wouldn't be traumatized if the courts awarded him to me instead of you. Kayla would have no choice but to witness that I saw Jake, and helped care for him, nearly every day since his birth."

Again Allie was silent. She seemed to be taking it all in, processing it. Liam watched as her face settled into a guarded, expressionless mask.

"You know what makes this really unforgivable, don't you?" she finally asked.

Liam did not respond. He knew exactly what she meant. He didn't have to say it out loud and in front of her ex-husband. He'd slept with her with this horrible secret between them. She could come to no other conclusion than he was the plotting, back-stabbing bastard Doug accused him of being. And if he hadn't decided last night to stop his adoption plans, they'd both be right.

He knew he was stupid and desperate to try, but Liam had to at least *attempt* to convince her that he would never have made love to her if he'd intended to continue scheming to adopt Jake.

"I know you aren't going to believe this, Allie, but last night I decided not to go through with the adoption plans."

Doug laughed sarcastically. "I suppose you made this decision just before you undressed her. Maybe now that she's got her clothes back on, you've changed your mind again."

"Shut up, Doug," Allie said, but without perceptible anger. "We might as well let him finish." She sighed and looked down at Jake, who was now sucking contentedly on his bottle. "So Liam, what *did* make you change your mind?"

"It was when I saw how upset you were about the accident."

"What accident?" Doug interrupted.

Allie held up her hand. "Please, Doug—" He retreated, scowling. She looked at Liam. "You could use the accident against me. You could say I was careless and irresponsible. That I'd put Jake in harm's way.''

Liam nodded. "Yes, I know. I thought of that. But when I came by the house and saw how distraught you were, I realized how much you love him, Allie. It finally hit me how cruel it would be to take him away from you…or even to make the attempt and fail. I know he belongs with you now. I won't do anything to stand in your way or make things difficult for you. I promise.''

Allie had fixed him with a dispassionate gaze during this whole last speech. Now she looked away, then down at Jake again. She said nothing, betrayed no emotions whatsoever. To see her glazed disillusionment and corresponding withdrawal into herself made Liam ache inside. He'd done this to her! He'd hurt her and she was adding him to her list of life's let-me-downs. Liam could see the list clearly…. There he was, right below Doug Renshaw, her last disappointment.

Liam stood up, collected his trench coat and walked to the door. "Despite everything, Allie, I really do appreciate you hooking your grandfather up with Bea. He's been a tremendous help and I'll always be grateful to you.'' Then he left, closing the door quietly behind him.

ALLIE WAS IN SHOCK. She watched the door close, then immediately stood up and carried Jake into his bedroom and laid him in his crib. Doug had silently trailed behind her, and now stood in the dark room, watching her. He was probably waiting for her to fall apart so he could pick up the pieces, she decided, vaguely annoyed but too tired to confront him about it.

"Do you want me to stay?"

She looked up from Jake's sweetly sleeping face and met Doug's eyes. She had to admit, he really did look concerned about her. He had his weaknesses—hell, didn't they all?—but she'd always believed he loved her. So, maybe he wasn't just waiting for a weak moment, an opportunity to pounce on her when she was too sad or lonely to resist him…after which he'd slowly and persistently insinuate himself back into her life. Maybe he truly wanted to help and console her for the pure reasons she thought she saw—she *hoped* she saw—reflected in his eyes. "Yes," she sighed. "Stay."

He closed his eyes on a prayer or an oath, took two steps and pulled her into his arms. Kissing her hair, he promised, "Don't worry, Allie, baby. I'm here for you."

Chapter Ten

Liam spent a sleepless night, then got up before everyone else in the morning and called his lawyer. Conrad Lewis was still in bed and groggy when he answered the phone—it was an hour earlier in California, plus it was a Saturday—but he snapped to attention when Liam explained that he'd changed his mind and was dropping his plans to adopt Jake.

"You've spent a hell of a lot of money for nothing, Mr. McAllister," he pointed out.

"I'm not worried about that," Liam replied. "Just send me the bill and it'll be promptly paid."

Mr. Lewis assured him that he would, and they hung up.

"Well, that was simple," Liam mumbled to himself. But he knew that what the rest of the day held in store was not going to be simple at all. Starting with his grandmother.

Liam retreated outside to the deck when he heard Mrs. Preedy and Ribchester descending the stairs, headed for the kitchen to cook up their usual hearty English breakfast. He was in no mood for friendly chitchat, and he couldn't eat a thing. He did crave a good hot cup of coffee, though.

It was nippy outside and Liam was wishing for his jacket when the sliding doors behind him opened and Ribchester stuck his head out. "Care for some coffee, my lord?"

Liam smiled. "You're a lifesaver, Ribchester. I'd love some coffee. But no breakfast this morning."

Ribchester frowned and seemed about to object and urge him to think better of such an unwise course of action. But then, after observing Liam's unshaven face, with the dark circles under his eyes, he held his tongue. He retreated, returning minutes later with the steaming mug of coffee and holding Liam's jacket out to him.

"I hope you don't mind, my lord, but I took the liberty—"

Liam smiled gratefully as he slipped on the jacket and took the coffee. "You're a good man, Ribchester."

Ribchester made a slight bow, but looked grim and aggravated as he closed the sliding doors behind him.

Minutes later, Liam heard the doors open again and this time his grandmother stepped onto the deck. Already dressed in tailored black slacks and a pale yellow sweater, she looked trim and casual, but still elegant. A smile wreathed her face and her eyes shone like jewels. The sight of her, so happy and radiant after her reunion with Jacob Lockwood the night before, made Liam sick with self-loathing. He had probably ruined this second chance of happiness for her.

Liam tried to put on a good face. "Good morning,

Gran. You look wonderful,'' he said in a voice as close to cheerful as he could manage. He nonchalantly lifted his coffee mug to his lips.

As she studied him, Mary's smile slipped away. "Sorry I can't return the compliment, Liam. You look like bloody hell."

Liam choked on his coffee. "Gran! That's pretty rough language coming from you!"

"Well, it's the truth. You don't look as though you've slept a wink. I thought Ribchester was exaggerating when he told me you looked blue deviled and cupshot, but he was right."

Liam laughed. "Good God, Gran. No one says 'blue deviled' and 'cupshot' anymore."

"Ribchester obviously does. And we both know exactly what he means. *Are* you depressed, and *did* you get drunk last night?"

"Yes, I am a little down, but no, I did not get drunk last night. Sounds like a good plan for *tonight,* though."

"What's going on with you, Liam? You've seemed so much happier lately, more content. And Bea's so much better, too. What could have happened since yesterday? The last I saw of you, you were towing Allie's car to her—"

Mary stopped abruptly, her eyes narrowing. "This is about Allie, isn't it? Are you two...er...involved, Liam?"

Liam sighed and sat down in a patio chair. Mary sat down opposite him, her eyes trained on his face. "That's a very difficult question to answer, Gran. But it needs to be answered. It will take a few minutes to explain everything, so I'd better get your jacket.''

Liam started to get up, but Ribchester, with his usual magical timing, showed up at the sliding doors with Mary's jacket.

"Excuse me, my lady, but it's really too nippy for you to be outside without this," he intoned apologetically.

Mary thanked him, Ribchester vanished, and Liam began his story. He managed to get through the explanation of his secret scheme to adopt Jake by avoiding Mary's eyes, which he feared would hold equal parts disappointment and despair. Disappointment in him, and despair that her relationship with Jacob would be ended before it had a chance to begin.

When Liam finally looked at Mary, the expression in her eyes surprised him. All he saw there was love and concern.

"I've been a fool. A jackass. A first-class jerk," he said, just to get the ball rolling. He deserved to be scolded.

"Yes," Mary agreed quietly. "It was wrong of you to keep your plans from everyone—especially Allie— but the emotional shape you were in when you arrived here excuses you a little. You fell in love with Jake and you wanted him to be part of your life...which has been lacking since you lost Victoria and the baby. You were trying to fill a vacant place in your heart."

"But I never really thought of it like that, Gran," Liam protested, leaning forward. "I never meant Jake to replace Victoria and the baby we lost. I knew no one ever could. I just thought it would be wonderful to have him in our lives. A son for me, a brother for Bea. And he needed a home, Gran. He'd been abandoned. I found him…*saved* him.''

''You saved him with Allie's help. And you know she was more than eager to give him a home, too, Liam,'' Mary reminded him firmly. ''You were very much in the wrong when it comes to your dealings with Allie. You should have been honest with her from the beginning, and given her a fair chance to prepare her own case for adopting Jake.''

''I tried not to think about being fair to Allie,'' Liam admitted. ''On an unconscious level I think I figured life hadn't been fair to me, so why should I be fair to anyone else? Besides, I rationalized that she'd be having her own babies someday, whereas I had no assurance that I'd find someone to love again, remarry, and have more children.''

Mary's brows lifted in surprise. ''Ah. Then you don't know? I didn't know, either, until Mrs. Preedy told me the other day. But I was sure *you* would have heard by now.''

Liam frowned. ''What are you talking about? What don't I know?''

Mary shook her head. ''Apparently it's common knowledge in Annabella that Allie is…well, she won't ever have her own children, Liam. Allie has some medical problems and she's infertile.''

Liam was stunned. He remembered last night when he'd mentioned needing the condom so she wouldn't get pregnant. She could have told him then that pregnancy was not a concern. Of course, maybe she figured the condom was a necessary precaution anyway, considering the media's exaggerated reports on his love life. But still, she could have told him then that it was impossible for her to get pregnant.

Having finally processed this new bit of insight about Allie, Liam was devastated. "Oh, Gran, what a shame. She'd make a wonderful mother."

"She's a wonderful mother already…to Jake."

"And I was going to try to ruin that for her," he groaned.

"You didn't know."

Liam sighed. "I'm not sure that would have made a difference in the beginning. I was determined."

"What made you change your mind, Liam? And so suddenly?"

"I'm not sure it was all that sudden. I saw last night that Allie obviously adores Jake, but I'd probably seen it before—seen it all along—and refused to acknowledge it to myself. She made a mistake when she left him in the car, but she couldn't forgive herself for the lapse of judgment. She's a quick learner, Gran, and I know she'll take good care of Jake from now on."

Mary nodded. "I agree. So that's settled, and you're all right about Jake? But you'll miss him when you go back to England."

"Of course I will."

"Is there anyone else you'll miss?"

Liam snatched a quick look at his grandmother's face, then just as quickly looked away. As usual, she was much sharper than he wanted her to be. He was reluctant to admit that he had feelings for Allie because, besides all the impediments that existed before she knew about his duplicities, she had every reason to hate him now. He was more concerned with how last night's revelations would affect his grandmother's life.

"Gran, it's time to talk about you. I'm a lost cause."

"Nonsense, Liam—"

"I feel terrible about how this is going to affect your relationship with Allie's grandfather."

Mary looked both surprised and embarrassed. "To begin with, Liam, I don't know why you call it a 're-lationship.' At this…er…point, I would rather call it a renewed 'friendship.' And I don't think our friendship is going to be the least bit influenced by this unfortunate business between you and Allie."

Liam sat up straighter. "You don't?"

"No. Why should it? It has nothing to do with Jacob and me." Her voice rose slightly and her tone was fervent. "I certainly don't intend to let it stand in the way of a continuing friendship with Jacob, and I would be extremely disappointed in him if he didn't feel the same way."

"Well, I hope he—"

"As you mature, Liam," she continued in a lecturing tone, "you learn to not let difficulties overwhelm a treasured friendship. You work *through* them." Seeming to realize she'd been as close to shouting as had ever occurred in her seventy-eight years on the earth, she added quietly and meekly, "Especially when you were stupid enough to let over fifty years pass by before mending hurt feelings and misunderstandings."

Liam said nothing. He simply sat and gazed at his

grandmother with admiration. She fidgeted a little and blushed. Finally he said, "So, are you and Jacob seeing each other again today?"

"Yes," she answered self-consciously. "I'm joining him and Bea in their session right after breakfast. That was the whole intention of our getting together in the first place...so I could join them, you know. It was at Bea's request."

Liam nodded. "Yes, I know. But you're glad something occurred to break the ice, aren't you?"

Mary smiled. "Yes. I'm very happy."

Liam just hoped Gran *stayed* happy. Call him a cynic, but he wasn't so sure Jacob Lockwood was going to show up for his appointment with Bea and Mary.

Fortunately, Liam was proved wrong.

Promptly at ten o'clock, the very hour to the very minute they'd settled on, Jacob was ushered by Ribchester into the great room.

Liam sat in a chair by the fire at the far end of the large room, neither trying to blend into the scenery nor push himself on Allie's grandfather. He was waiting for Jacob's reaction before deciding what to do. Now that he knew Jacob wasn't going to let Liam's problems with Allie affect his friendship with Mary and Bea, he wanted to apologize, but wasn't sure this was the proper time or place.

As it happened, Liam had plenty of time to think about the situation before Jacob ever noticed him. Bea ran to him when he first entered the room and he stooped to exchange several kind and friendly words with her, then turned his eyes to Mary.

Liam was startled by the expression that spread over Jacob's aging, but still handsome, features. *My God,* Liam thought, *he still loves her!* And the warmth in Mary's eyes didn't fall too short of the ardor in his!

It occurred to Liam that he ought to feel jealous or offended for his dead grandfather's sake, but he knew that Mary had loved only Cecil during their long and happy marriage. For Mary to rekindle a love she'd known as a girl—if that was, indeed, happening— didn't seem the least disloyal to him. In Liam's estimation, the fact that Mary was brave enough to risk loving again said volumes about the happiness she'd shared with his grandfather. It took courage to give your heart away…courage that could only develop from trusting relationships and happy memories.

"Liam? Where are your manners? Say hello to our guest."

Mary's voice broke into Liam's runaway thoughts. He stood up and walked across the long room to stand before Jacob Lockwood. The man looked at him sternly, but didn't throw a punch. Liam found this encouraging.

Liam didn't want to bring up the whole mess in front of Bea, but he did want to be as straightforward with Jacob as possible. "I wasn't sure you'd want to say hello to me," Liam ventured.

"I wasn't sure, either, young man," Jacob admitted in a quiet voice. "But, for Mary and Bea's sake, I'm willing to give you the benefit of the doubt and believe you'd already changed your mind about—" He stopped and glanced at Bea, as aware as Liam that they couldn't be as open as they'd like. "*—things,* before Doug showed up last night. I'm just glad you aren't going through with it."

Bea skipped away to put on the coat Mrs. Preedy was holding open for her, and Jacob took the opportunity to lean closer and say, "Just promise me you won't do anything else to upset my granddaughter."

"I do promise." And having said that, Liam couldn't figure out a better way to keep his promise than to stay away from Allie completely. The idea was daunting. It made him more miserable than he could ever have imagined.

"Thank you for continuing to work with Bea," Liam said. "That means more to me than you'll ever know."

Jacob gave a curt nod. "Oh, I think I know."

While Mary and Bea walked happily out the door with Jacob, Liam contemplated a lonely afternoon. He wondered what Allie was doing on her day off. He wondered if Doug had stayed the night with her....

Liam couldn't stand the jealous knot that twisted in his stomach at the idea of Doug comforting Allie, perhaps taking advantage of her. After pacing the floor for several minutes, he finally threw on a Levi's jacket and went outside with the intention of chopping enough wood for the fireplace to last through the winter.

ALLIE WOKE to the sound of the shower going in her bathroom. The door was open and steam was escaping into the bedroom. She groaned and turned over. She hoped Doug would leave her enough hot water so she wouldn't have to freeze through another skimpy

shower. When they were married he *always* hogged
the hot water—

Allie sat up abruptly. What was Doug doing using
her shower? For one frightening moment, she was
afraid to remember. But, no, it was okay. Doug stayed
the night, but he'd slept on the couch, and there was
no reason why he couldn't have used the other bathroom down the hall.

Suddenly the shower stopped and Allie pulled her
blanket up to her chin. Maybe an attempt at modesty
was ridiculous, considering they were married for five
years, but she had no intention of giving Doug the
wrong idea.

Doug stepped out of the bathroom with a towel
around his trim waist. When he saw Allie was awake
and watching, he grinned at her as he ran his fingers
through his thick, wet hair. Doug had always had a
wonderful head of hair.

"Morning, Allie. Just like old times, isn't it?"

"If you mean you've probably used up all the hot
water, I guess that qualifies for 'like old times.' But I
wouldn't call it one of my fondest memories of our
marriage," Allie answered dryly.

Doug cocked a brow. "So you admit to having
some fond memories, do you?"

Allie knew what he was hinting at. They'd always
had a great sex life...until everything fell apart.
She gave her ex-husband a once-over. This was the
first time she'd seen him nearly naked since the divorce. He was still a hunk...with that sculpted chest
and slim hips, and no trace of a gut. His hair was
always glossy and extra wavy when wet, as now. He

was fresh-shaven—he must have used her razor—and she could smell his warm, soap-scented masculinity as he stood close to the bed.

"Tempted, Allie?" he asked her with a provocative glint in his blue eyes.

Allie was almost sorry she *wasn't* tempted. Doug was attractive and a good lover, but Liam McAllister had been in her bed last night and her mind and heart was full of *him.* His kisses, his lovemaking had taken her beyond the physical pleasures—although that part had been wonderful…even better than with Doug— but her heart had been touched in a way she'd never experienced before.

In short, it was entirely possible that Liam had ruined her for *all* other men, not just her ex.

"Doug," Allie began, wanting to let him down easy. After all, he'd been so sweet to her last night and hadn't put the moves on her once. "I—"

"Never mind, Allie," Doug interrupted. "I know that tone of voice. The answer's no. You're not even tempted."

He sounded so deflated, so sad, Allie felt awful. "Doug, it's not that you're not attractive. You know you are—"

"Only not to you. Not anymore."

Allie said nothing. He was right.

Doug leaned a bare shoulder against the wall and sighed deeply. "It was stupid of me, but I was hoping when you finally got the baby you'd always wanted, there'd be a chance for us again."

Allie nodded. "I was afraid you were thinking that.

But our problems went far deeper than the infertility issue.''

"You mean that thing with Rhonda Middleburger, don't you?'' he said bitterly. "Hell, Allie, you were always pushing me away—''

"*Always,* Doug?'' Allie shook her head vigorously. "You know that's not true. And if I was sad and not feeling especially sexy right after finding out I didn't have all the right equipment to make babies, it sure as hell didn't help to find out you'd been cheating on me!''

Doug raked a hand through his wet hair. "God, Allie, you don't know how sorry I am that I made you feel that way! You're beautiful and desirable and everything a man could want. If only you could forgive me for that one indiscretion—!''

"If only it *had* been just the one indiscretion.''

Doug's face flooded with color. "What makes you think—''

"Listen to me, Doug,'' Allie interrupted. "For the sake of all we meant to each other at one time, and for the sake of the friendship I hope we'll always have, just admit it.''

He closed his eyes and gritted his teeth. She could see the muscles working in his jaws.

More gently, she continued, "Admit that there was more than one affair, Doug.''

"They weren't 'affairs.' I never cared for anyone but—''

"Women you slept with, then. There were several, weren't there.'' Even more gently, she urged, "For once, Doug, tell the truth.''

When Doug opened his eyes, they were moist with emotion. "I never meant to hurt you, Allie."

Allie nodded, her own eyes filling with tears. "I know."

AT ELEVEN O'CLOCK, Ribchester called to Liam from the deck. "There's a phone call, my lord. It's Sheriff Renshaw, and he says it's urgent."

Wiping the sweat off his brow with the back of his forearm, Liam started for the house. *What does that bastard want?* he grumbled to himself. Then he began to worry that something might have happened to Gran or Bea...or Allie. He jogged up the dirt path, entered through the kitchen and grabbed the portable phone Ribchester held out for him.

"Renshaw? What's the matter?"

"Calm down, McAllister. No one's hurt. I don't know why that's the first conclusion everyone jumps to when they get a call from an officer of the law...."

Liam breathed a sign of relief. "Cut the crap, Renshaw, just tell me why you're calling."

"There's been a breakthrough on the Jake case."

"What do you mean a 'breakthrough'? Did you find the mother?" *And why are you calling me?*

"I'm at my office. Your grandmother and your daughter are both here. So's Doctor Lockwood and Allie. I think you should come down, too."

Liam couldn't fathom what he was hearing. "*What?* What are Gran and Bea doing down there? Renshaw, what the hell is going on?"

"Just get down here, okay? I haven't got time for

this.'' Then he hung up. Liam stared at the phone for a minute, puzzled and angry.

''What's the matter, my lord?'' Mrs. Preedy asked in a quavery voice. Liam could see that both Mrs. Preedy and Ribchester were alarmed.

''Has something happened to Bea or your grandmother?'' Ribchester demanded to know.

Liam shook his head and put his hand on Mrs. Preedy's shoulder. ''No, they're fine,'' he assured them both. ''But, for some reason, they're down at the sheriff's office and I've been summoned, as well. It's got something to do with the investigation into Jake's abandonment.''

The elderly servants' eyes widened. ''Well... goodness,'' Ribchester said, rather inadequately.

''Don't worry. Renshaw's probably yanking our chains, making himself look important,'' Liam told them, grabbing a paper towel and wiping at the sweat and dirt on his face as he headed toward the door. Abruptly he turned around. ''Why don't you drive me down, Ribchester, and I'll send Bea home with you? We might be discussing stuff that Bea shouldn't hear.''

Ribchester immediately removed his apron, grabbed the keys to Mary's Lincoln Continental from a hook on the wall, and followed Liam out the door.

''Excuse me, my lord,'' Ribchester said as they walked to the car. ''What does 'yanking one's chains' mean, exactly?''

Liam explained the American slang term as best he could while Ribchester drove sedately down the

mountain. Liam was wishing he'd had the forethought
to insist on driving. Ten long minutes later, Ribchester
pulled the car into a diagonal parking space in front
of the sheriff's tiny office.

"Wait here, Ribchester," Liam ordered, then he got
out and strode quickly to the door. As he entered, five
pair of eyes turned in his direction. Jake was asleep in
his carrier on the floor, carefully placed out of the way
so he wouldn't be tripped over. Everyone else was
circled around a table, over which was spread the quilt
Jake had been wrapped in when Liam found him.

Liam's eyes met Allie's first, saw too many emotions reflected there to even begin to recognize or label
them, then shifted his gaze to Bea and his grandmother.

The emotions in Mary's eyes were easier to read.
They were full of trouble and confusion. All the more
reason to get Bea out of there.

"I'm sending Bea home with Ribchester," he announced to everyone collectively, then he took Bea to
a corner of the room and put his arm around her. She
looked up at him with big, curious eyes. He wasn't
sure if she understood everything going on, but she
was definitely picking up on the tension.

"Busy Bea, Mrs. Preedy needs your help at home
to fix a special dessert for dinner. Do you mind?"

"No, I don't mind," she readily replied. Then she
leaned close and whispered, "You will tell me what
you find out later, won't you, Daddy?"

Liam smiled. "You're not buying the story about
the dessert, are you?"

"I know you want to get rid of me, and that you

think it's for my own good," Bea answered, then she shrugged good-naturedly. "So I don't mind. You probably know best."

Liam ignored the "probably" part and gave Bea an affectionate squeeze. "You *are* a very intelligent girl. And I do promise to explain everything later. Now come along."

Liam walked Bea outside and put her in the car, fastened her seat belt, kissed her cheek and waved goodbye as Ribchester backed out of the parking spot and drove away at his usual snail's pace.

Liam reentered the office and went directly to his grandmother. He took her by the shoulders and asked urgently, "What's wrong, Gran? What's going on?"

"The quilt, Liam," Mary quavered.

"What about it?"

"It's…it's *mine*, Liam."

Chapter Eleven

Allie had watched with an anxious heart the first time Liam strode into the office. She'd observed him while he talked to his daughter. He looked terrible. He was unshaven and appeared as though he'd spent a sleepless night, judging by those dark circles under his eyes. His face was smeared with dirt and sawdust and his skin glistened with sweat. Instead of an English aristocrat, he looked like a manual laborer just home from the sawmill. But despite the haggard eyes and disheveled hair, he looked just as sexy as usual. Well, no, maybe even sexier…

Allie reined in her wayward thoughts and reminded herself that Liam was a lying sneak. Sure, he'd supposedly repented at the last minute, but how would she ever know for sure that he'd truly intended to call off his bid to adopt Jake before Doug showed up, armed with evidence? Had he really made love to her with a clear conscience, or had he made love to her still intending to steal her baby away from her?

Seeing Liam again brought all these hurtful thoughts to the forefront, but Allie had more important matters to deal with at the moment. Liam had just come back from taking Bea to the car and found out what Allie had only known herself for about thirty minutes. The quilt had been recognized and claimed by—of all people in the world—Mary McAllister!

"The quilt is yours, Gran?" Liam repeated incredulously. "Are you sure?"

"We were walking by the office when I looked in and saw the quilt," Mary began. "I didn't recognize it right away. I didn't have my glasses on and couldn't see it clearly. But Jacob—" Mary's voice suddenly choked up.

"It was the first time I'd got a good look at it, too," Jacob said, quickly picking up where Mary left off. "Some of the patches caught my eye immediately."

Jacob pointed to a patch with a pale pink gingham background covered with tiny purple pansies. "Mary wore that dress to a church picnic just after we got engaged. It was a pinafore, and she wore it with a white blouse that had short, fluffy sleeves."

He pointed to another patch, dark blue with flecks of silvery white. "Mary wore that dress to a school dance. It was kind of swirly at the bottom and had shoulder pads like those dresses Bette Davis and Katharine Hepburn wore in the movies. Mary was always a bit of a fashion plate, you know. It was the night I asked her to go steady."

Allie stared, dumbstruck, at her grandfather. She felt she should be a little jealous for her grandmother's sake. "I'm amazed you remember all this, Gramps."

Jacob continued to study the quilt. "Oh, given enough time, I'd probably remember every dress or pair of pedal-pushers these patches represent." He eagerly pointed to another patch. "Mary, isn't that the dress you made for your mother to wear on Mother's Day in '39? I distinctly recall helping you pick out the fabric at the JCPenney in Kamas."

Mary gave a watery chuckle. Her eyes were swimming in tears. "As *I* recall, Jacob, you weren't much help."

They both laughed and a tear got loose and ran down Mary's cheek. Eventually the two former sweethearts seemed to remember that they weren't the only people in the room, and Mary blushed and apologized. "Sorry I'm such a watering pot. I'm just feeling a little sentimental, that's all."

Sentimental, and probably incredibly touched and flattered, thought Allie. Obviously her grandfather had once loved Mary very much…and appeared to be well on his way to falling in love with her again. She glanced at Liam and wondered what he thought about these two lovebirds.

"So, are we just going on Jacob's word here?" Doug finally spoke up. Allie was surprised that he hadn't interrupted earlier. "Or do you definitely recognize the quilt as yours, Mrs. McAllister? We can't just depend on Jacob's identification of the patches as having once been items of clothing belonging to you."

Mary nodded firmly. "Oh, the quilt's mine, all right. I just had to get a good look at it. My mother and I pieced it together during those first few months Jacob was away at war."

"But how did it end up wrapped around Jake?" Liam wondered out loud.

"That's what we have to figure out," Doug answered. "I'll have to ask you a few questions, Mrs. McAllister. And I might as well begin now. Why don't you get comfortable in this chair here, and I'll get you whatever you need." Doug took Mary's arm and led her to a chair by his desk. "Would you like some water? Coke? Or do you want tea? That's what you Brits like, isn't it?"

"Wait a minute," Liam said, with his hands in the air. "Not so fast. Does my grandmother need a lawyer?"

"You *would* ask that, wouldn't you?" Doug said in a beleaguered tone. "Look, if you're asking me if I think your grandmother had something to do with Jake's birth and abandonment, or wondering if I'm trying to somehow pin it on her, the answer is *hell* no."

"Okay," Allie soothed. "Let's keep things professional and not let personal feelings intrude." She gave Doug a significant look. "We all want the same thing here. We want the truth, and that will take cooperation from everyone."

"I'm willing to cooperate," Mary said, sitting down. She'd sniffed away her last tear and stashed her handkerchief in her sweater pocket. "I'm as eager as anyone to come to the bottom of this mystery. Especially now that I'm strangely linked to it. And I don't need water, Coke *or* tea, thank you."

That being said, everyone found seats in the little office and trained their eyes on Mary. She appeared completely composed now and didn't seem the least bit intimidated, but then she had no fear of the truth.

If there was some involvement on her part in Jake's abandonment, it was indirect and innocent.

Allie wished she was as comfortable as Mary. She dreaded the truth. She had a sinking feeling that the truth was somehow going to take away her baby. She looked at Jake, still peacefully sleeping in his carrier, and fear squeezed her heart like a fist.

Doug sat behind his desk and leaned over it toward Mary, his hands clasped together in front of him. He looked very Sheriff-like, very intent on getting to that damned truth.

"Mrs. McAllister, when was the last time you saw the quilt?"

Mary frowned, thinking hard. "I'm trying to remember."

"Did you take it to England with you, Gran?"

Doug scowled at Liam. His look said *he* wanted to conduct the interrogation, thank you very much, so *shut up.* Liam scowled back.

"I didn't take it when I went to England the first time," Mary said. "You know, when I went as a WAC and met Cecil."

"So, it remained here at your parents' house?"

"Yes." Now Mary's memory seemed to be coming back. "Yes, that's right. Then, years later, when my mother passed away and I came home to help Father with the funeral, I went through a few old trunks and boxes."

"And you came across the quilt again?"

"Yes. I took it home to England with me. I gave it to my girls. For their dolls, you know." She smiled wistfully, a fond memory absorbing her for a moment. "I had three girls and just one boy. Liam's father."

"Right," Doug said tersely. "So, if you gave it to your daughters to play with in England, how'd it end up back here?"

"Well, let me think...." Her brow cleared. "Oh, yes. Of course. When Father passed on, I inherited the property with the stone cottage where my parents retired to—the property where I live now."

Doug nodded. "Yes. And?"

"And I remember bringing the quilt back to America, a bit tattered now, but holding more sentimental value for me than ever. I decided it *belonged* in Utah. I put it away for safekeeping."

"Where exactly did you put it? Think hard, Mrs. McAllister," Doug urged.

"In the trunk in the cottage," she said with a decided and satisfied nod of her head. "Yes, that's it. I put it in the cedar trunk at the foot of the bed."

"In the cottage, not the cabin where you live now?"

"One can hardly call what I live in now a *cabin*, can one?" she observed. "Although Cecil insisted on doing so."

"Mrs. McAllister—"

"As I said, I put the quilt in the trunk in the *cottage*, Sheriff Renshaw."

"Do you remember taking the quilt out of the trunk, Mrs. McAllister?" Doug was getting impatient, excited. If it was possible to shake the facts out of Mary McAllister, he'd have probably taken her by her dainty ankles and turned her upside down.

"No, I don't remember taking it out."

"Well, *someone* took it out of the trunk. It didn't just walk out on its own."

For several tense moments, Mary thought intently. Finally she looked up and shrugged helplessly. "I don't remember ever seeing it again after I stashed it away. I'd quite forgotten the dear old thing. Goodness, it's been years—"

"Twenty years."

Everyone turned and looked at Liam, startled.

"What did you say?" Allie gasped.

"I said the last time Gran saw the quilt was twenty years ago," Liam stated evenly, his expression grim.

"How do you know that, McAllister?" Doug demanded, rising to his feet and glowering at him over the desk.

"Because *I* was the one who took it out of the trunk."

Suddenly Mary was no longer the center of attention. Allie, and everyone else, stared at Liam. They waited for him to speak, to reveal the contents of the Pandora's box he'd just opened.

And was it really a Pandora's box, with all kinds of horrible things inside, Allie wondered? Was Liam's revelation going to be detrimental to her hope of adopting Jake? Was *Liam* going to be the reason she lost her baby, after all?

"*You* took the quilt out of the trunk," Doug repeated carefully. "But I thought you'd never seen it before!"

"I didn't remember seeing it before, but I do now."

"What the hell does that mean?" Doug growled.

"I'd forgotten about it. I only saw it once."

"When you took it out of the trunk?"

"Yes."

"Twenty years ago?"

"Yes, when I was thirteen years old, visiting Gran."

"Are you sure you're remembering right? That was a long time ago."

"I'm positive."

Doug sat down slowly, then leaned forward, his gaze intense as he seemed to be trying to stare down Liam. His mouth formed a disbelieving smirk. "All right, McAllister. If you're so damned sure you're remembering right, tell us why you took the quilt out of the trunk in the first place. You weren't playing with dolls, were you? What did you do with it?"

Liam turned away from Doug and rested a sad gaze on each of them in turn...first Mary, then Jacob, then Allie. Allie's heart went to her throat. She was frightened. And, despite everything, she felt compassion for Liam. Clearly he was anguished about what he remembered and what he was about to reveal. And Allie knew instinctively that, in a few minutes, she was going to feel just as sick at heart.

Liam sighed, turned to stare through the window at the sunny fall day outside, and began his story. "She'd been underfoot all day. Tom and Jerry and I had been trying to build a trench. We were playing soldiers. The Brits against the Germans. Kayla had her dolls, as usual. She dragged around two or three at a time, playing house. She always wanted me to play with her. She knew better than to ask her brothers. I guess they got their fill of Kayla's entreaties to 'play house' at home. Sometimes they'd get impatient with her and yell at her to get lost, or go back to the house. I felt sorry for her. But I wanted her out of our hair, too. I thought maybe if I got her something to play with—''

Mary made a small sound of distress and pressed her hand against her mouth. Jacob drew near and put his arm around her.

''I wasn't sure what I was looking for when I went into the cottage. Gran didn't let us play in there. She had some things put away for 'safekeeping,' she said. I opened the trunk at the foot of the bed and rummaged around till I found the quilt. I decided it would be perfect for Kayla to use for her dolls...which she tended to drag around half naked. She loved it. She went off and sat down under a tree, cooing and cuddling her babies in that quilt. It worked. She quit bugging us and we built our trench.''

In the silence that followed Liam's story, Allie recreated that summer day in her mind's eye. She saw it all. Or rather she saw it *again,* just as it happened twenty years ago. Just as she witnessed it from her hideaway high in the cottonwood tree. Swift and sure, the anguish she'd been expecting and dreading, consumed her.

''Are you trying to tell me you think Kayla is Jake's mother?'' Doug's tone was incredulous.

''All I'm saying is that I gave the quilt to Kayla.''

Doug shot to his feet. ''No, that's not all you're saying. You're saying Kayla's the most likely person to be Jake's mother! But your evidence—if you can call it that!—is flimsy at best. No one can corroborate your so-called memory, so—''

"I can corroborate it," Allie said dully. "I saw it all, just the way Liam described it. I was watching from the cottonwood tree. I watched every day while Liam was visiting Mary."

Now Doug turned on Allie. "What's the matter with you, Allie? Are you so hot for this guy, you'd lie for him? How can you let him accuse your sister of doing such a horrible thing?"

"She's not lying for me, Renshaw," Liam said. "Even Kayla will tell you that Allie spent her days watching us from the cottonwood tree."

"I saw her up there once, too," Mary said quietly.

Doug released a hiss of frustration. "I find it hard to believe that you people are entertaining the idea—"

"You've been dead set on solving this case since Liam found Jake," Jacob said. "Now you seem dead set on not seeing what's right in front of your nose. We're not saying we know for sure Kayla's Jake's mother, but it's a lead, and a damned compelling one. You need to follow up on it."

"My guess is Kayla gave that quilt to the Goodwill," Doug grumbled.

"Goodwill takes the donations they've collected in town and transports them miles away," Jacob said.

"How do you know that?"

"I used to volunteer for the Goodwill, Doug. You might as well accept the fact that that quilt has stayed here in Annabella for the last twenty years. And Kayla was the last person, that we know of, who had the quilt in her possession."

Doug sat down, propped his elbows on the desk and held his head in his hands. "How could she have been pregnant and none of us know it?" He lifted his head and stared at Allie. "How could *you* not notice it, Allie? You're her sister. Hell, you're a *doctor*."

Allie bit her lip and shook her head helplessly. "I don't know. She hasn't felt well for months, but I chalked that up to the stress in her life. She's always been moody. And I didn't really notice much change in her body...although it's hard to see her shape at all in those baggy sweats she wears. When she was carrying Travis, she didn't look that pregnant, either. She just looked heavier. I *did* notice that she seemed to have lost weight lately, but I didn't say anything because that would imply that I'd noticed she'd *gained* weight over the summer. She's so sensitive, you know."

"She could have carried a child without anyone knowing," Jacob concurred.

"But if Kayla's the mother—" Allie looked at Doug. "And I do mean *if,* because nothing's been proven...who's the father? As far as I know, she hasn't seen Brad for over a year. And Kayla's not the type to jump in the sack with just anyone. Her self-image has been so crummy lately, I can't picture her getting intimate with a man at all." Something horrible suddenly occurred to Allie. "Oh, God, you don't think she was raped?"

"Okay, now we're getting carried away," Liam said carefully. "We don't know anything yet. All we know for sure is that I gave Kayla the quilt when she was five years old. Anything could have happened to it since then." Liam spoke to Allie. "You two grew up together. Do you remember seeing the quilt after that day?''

Allie shook her head. ''I don't know. I don't think so. She kept a little hoard of things under her bed. Things she didn't share or show to anyone else. Maybe it was in there. Besides, Kayla and I were several years apart and I was a tomboy. I didn't play with dolls.''

Suddenly everything seemed to be said. Silence fell over the group again, everyone nursing their own painful thoughts. Mary excused herself and went outside for a breath of fresh air. Jacob offered to go with her, worry etched on his face, but she'd refused with a grateful smile; she just wanted to be alone for a couple of minutes.

Eventually Liam, Jacob and Allie all turned to Doug. Allie was surprised he'd stayed quiet for so long. He sat with his head in his hands again, his face hidden.

Allie got a shiver down her back. His posture was so despairing. ''Doug?''

Doug looked up. His eyes were bleak, his face pale. ''I saw Kayla's car that night, going down Main. About eleven-thirty. I figured she was just driving Travis around, trying to get him to sleep, as usual. She waved at me—or motioned to me, I don't know which. But I drove on. I figured she wanted to talk, to flirt. You know how she is.''

''You saw her?'' Allie repeated, her throat gone dry. She realized then that she'd been desperately hoping their speculation would amount to nothing more than just that…speculation.

''The time fits,'' Jacob said thoughtfully. ''She

could have had the baby between the time Doug saw her and Liam found Jake in the Dumpster.''

"What kind of car does she drive?" Liam asked.

"An old Volvo station wagon," Doug answered. "Why? Do you remember seeing it at the station that night?"

"Is it a kind of steel blue?" Liam's facial expression showed that he clearly hoped it wasn't. That his emerging memory of that night was incorrect.

"Yes," said Jacob, the despair in his voice mirroring how they all felt.

"But who's the father?" Allie blurted, frustrated. "You can't get pregnant without a sperm donor, last I heard. I just don't think Kayla's been with anyone."

"She's been with someone," Doug stated flatly.

Again all eyes turned to Doug.

"She's been with me," he said miserably. "Just once. Ten months ago. I'd just received the final divorce papers. I went to Kayla's. She consoled me. We got drunk. We...we had sex. *Unprotected* sex."

Allie stared at her ex-husband. Up till then she'd been holding on. She'd subdued the anguish, the hysteria, the shock of everything she'd learned and suspected that night. She was losing Jake, one way or the other, which was almost more than she could bear. But to learn that her sister might be Jake's mother, that Kayla might be so emotionally damaged she'd throw away her own child, and now to find out that Doug was probably Jake's father.... It was too much.

The room faded to gray, then exploded in a blinding flash of white. She realized she was fainting...and was glad.

LIAM CAUGHT ALLIE as she pitched, headfirst, toward the floor. He sprang from his chair so quickly, it toppled over. The sharp thud as the chair hit the hardwood floor woke up the baby. Frightened, Jake screamed bloody murder.

Liam had Allie's head cradled in his lap and Jacob had gone to fetch a cold washcloth and a drink of water for her. Doug seemed frozen to his seat, looking back and forth between Allie and the baby, stupefied and distraught.

"Go pick him up," Liam ordered.

Doug blinked. "You mean...the baby?"

"Who the hell else would I mean?" Liam snapped.

Doug nodded, apparently too shocked by the afternoon's events to be offended by Liam's tone of voice. He staggered to his feet, propped his knuckles on the desk for a moment till he'd steadied himself, then walked across the room to where Jake was squirming and crying in his baby carrier.

While Liam stroked Allie's hair and murmured soothing words, he watched Doug pick up Jake. Despite his dislike of Doug—engendered mostly by their mutual jealousy of each other—Liam felt compassion for the man. This was the first time he would hold Jake, knowing he was his father. He didn't think Doug had really paid much attention to the baby up till now. He'd been consumed with solving the crime, of course, and probably hoping that Allie's adoption of a baby would help him get back together with her. But now he would be looking at Jake with new eyes. A father's eyes.

Jacob was back with something even better than a

cold washcloth. "I found this in a first-aid kit," he said, then waved a small ammonia stick under Allie's nose.

Allie's head jerked away from the strong smell, then her eyes opened. "Jake?" she murmured.

"He's all right," Liam assured her. And he was. Doug had somehow managed to quiet the baby without a bottle or a binky. He was walking him up and down the floor, gently bouncing him in his arms, singing a strange little lullaby. *"Hi - dumma - do - dumma, hi - dumma - diddle - dumma. Hi - dumma - diddle - dumma - day."*

Allie struggled to sit up. "That's my song," she objected weakly. "That's *my* baby."

"Hey, take it easy, hon," Jacob advised her. "You're still as pale as a ghost. You might pass out again."

But Allie wasn't listening. She was going to sit up come hell or high water, so Liam helped her. Once sitting upright, she pressed her hand against her forehead and swayed from side to side. "The room's spinning."

"Of course it is, you stubborn little fool," Jacob admonished her. "Lie down!"

Liam knew she wouldn't lie down again, so he pulled her against his chest. He could feel her stiffening, so he said, "Just think of me as a prop till you're over the dizziness." He leaned close to her ear and whispered, "Just a prop, Allie. That's all."

He heard her sigh softly and then she relaxed against him. He wanted to wrap his arms around her, but was pretty sure she wouldn't stand for that.

Mary walked in just then and stared, wide-eyed. "What happened?"

"Allie fainted," Jacob told her.

"But she was just fine when I left—"

"That's before she found out that Doug is Jake's father," Jacob informed her tersely.

Mary pressed her open palm to her chest and took a sharp intake of breath. "What can I do to help?" she asked in the next breath, always stalwart in an emergency.

"Things appear to be under control for the moment," Liam said, watching Doug handling Jake with surprising ease. He couldn't see Allie's face, but he could just imagine what she was thinking, how she was feeling as she watched Doug with Jake. She'd been unable to have a baby with Doug, but now, suddenly, he was a father. Only the baby's mother was her younger sister....

"When was the last time you ate, Allie?" Jacob asked her.

Allie shook her head, mumbled, "I don't know."

"She ate last night about eight o'clock," Liam offered. "But I don't know if she's eaten since then."

"I haven't," Allie admitted.

"Well then, you'd better eat something now."

"I'm not hungry."

"I don't care," Jacob informed her. "This day isn't nearly over yet, and you're going to need some nourishment so's you don't faint again."

"But I couldn't eat a—"

"Mary?" Jacob looked up at his old sweetheart, standing nearby and ready for orders. "Will you hop

over to Parson's Bakery and get Allie a sweet roll?
She likes those cream-cheese and lemon ones. She
needs some sugar in her blood.''

"Should I get some orange juice, too?''

"Doug's got some in his fridge.''

Mary hurried away and Jacob got the orange juice.
Allie drank it, seeming to realize that it would be useless to refuse. And perhaps she understood, as they all
did, that she'd need her strength for whatever the rest
of the day held in store.

After eating half the sweet roll, Allie was allowed
to stand up and she managed just fine. The whole time,
though, she'd been watching Doug with Jake. With
Mary's assistance, Doug had changed Jake's diaper
and fed him a bottle of formula. Now, still in Doug's
arms, Jake was happily looking about the room and
blowing bubbles.

Allie made no effort to take Jake away from Doug.
She just stood and stared at the two of them together,
her beautiful brown eyes muddy with misery. Liam
wanted so badly to comfort her, but he didn't dare.
She seemed to have built a protective shield around
herself, and he was the last person she'd allow past
that shield.

Doug didn't seem to know how to feel or behave.
He held Jake and gazed at him with a sort of awe
mixed with anxiety and confusion. When he looked at
Allie and saw her pain, it was obvious he felt it, too.
The remorse he felt for hurting her was written all over
his face. And, because of that, Liam found a smidgen
of forgiveness for him.

Finally Allie asked what they'd all been wondering.
"What's going to happen to Kayla?''

Chapter Twelve

"Before we even discuss that, we need to see Kayla," Doug answered, looking at the floor. "Talk to her. Find out what she really...*understands* about that night. She acts like she's in denial."

Allie was surprised that Doug seemed well informed about these kinds of cases. It wasn't like they'd had anything even similar happen in Annabella before. "You're right. She *could* be in denial. She might not even think of Jake as hers."

Doug nodded, still looking at the floor. "I haven't seen a lot of her. I've been avoiding her as much as possible since that night. I can't believe she's actually been baby-sitting Jake." He shook his head. "Why would she toss him in the Dumpster, then agree to take care of him for Allie? This is too weird."

"We need answers, and the only way we're going to get them is to go to Kayla's," Liam said. "I suggest we go right away."

Allie snatched a glance at Liam, who hovered nearby, as if afraid she'd keel over again and he wanted to stay close enough to catch her. His kindness during her fainting spell and its aftermath had warmed and sustained her. His respectful restraint had frustrated her…but she was glad for it now.

While she instinctively felt compelled to lean on him, and yearned for Liam's support and comfort, she knew she shouldn't. Her brain was in a muddle, she couldn't think straight and she needed to use what brain function she had to deal with Kayla's problem. Because that's what it all boiled down to. Kayla had one big problem, and Jake was in the middle of it.

What's going to happen to my baby? Allie's heart cried out. But he wasn't hers anymore.

"I agree, we should go to Kayla's right away," Jacob said. "But I'd like to take Mary home first, and I suggest she take Jake with her. Things are going to get pretty intense, and I don't think Jake should be there. Agreed?"

Jacob wasn't asking Allie. He was asking Doug. Already the source of parental authority had shifted, she thought dully.

Then Jacob turned to Mary. "You don't mind watching him, do you? I think he'd be better off with you till we get this sorted out."

Mary readily agreed. She wanted to help in any way she could.

They all climbed in Doug's car and transported Mary and Jake to her house, then the remaining four traveled the short distance to Kayla's. As they stopped in front of the house, no one seemed eager to get out.

"Timing-wise, this is good," Allie said on a positive note. "If Kayla can get Travis down for a nap, it's usually about this time of the afternoon."

"If he's not sleeping, I'll take him out back while

you guys talk to Kayla,'' Liam offered. ''He knows me and we get along great.''

No one objected to this plan, and since there was no longer any excuse to hesitate, they got out of the car and walked up to Kayla's door. Doug knocked and, shortly after, Kayla opened the door. The surprise on her face when she saw all four of them on her porch—an unlikely group to be together, that's for sure—was so quickly followed by unsuspicious delight, for a second Allie allowed herself to hope that Kayla couldn't possibly be Jake's mother.

''Wow. What brings all of you to *my* house? And all at the same time! It's like a party!'' She ushered them in, bustling and happy to have company. Allie realized with a pang of remorse how lonely her sister's life must be most of the time.

''Travis is asleep, thank God. He was up till two this morning. I'm a little low in the refreshment department right now. All I've got are some Fig Newtons and root beer. Fig Newtons are a healthy cookie, you know. I've been trying to cut down on the sugary stuff, for Travis's sake *and* mine—'' Suddenly she stopped, finally aware that none of them seemed as delighted by this visit as she was.

She scolded teasingly. ''Hey, what's with all the gloomy faces? You're not here to read me the riot act for feeding Jake some mashed bananas, are you? I only gave him a teaspoon, just a taste, really. I know he's a bit young for solid food, but he's such a hungry little bugger.''

She took a quick look around their sober-faced circle. ''Where is Jake, anyway?'' Her smile vanished and she quickly became agitated. "He's not sick, is he? Or hurt? Is that why you guys look so down?"

Jacob stepped forward and put his arm around Kayla, leading her to the couch. "Jake is just fine. He's spending the afternoon with Mary."

Naturally Kayla looked confused. "Mary? You mean, Mary McAllister? What for? Has she ever watched him before? If she's a total stranger to him, he might be frightened. If you wanted someone to watch him, why didn't you bring him here?"

Jacob and Allie sat down on either side of Kayla, and Liam sat down in the chair opposite the couch. Doug remained standing, his arms crossed loosely over his chest, his legs slightly spread, his knees locked. He didn't look threatening, just dead serious.

"We wanted to talk to you, Kayla," Doug said. "And we thought it best if Mary kept Jake till we were through."

Kayla shook her head confusedly and gave a nervous chuckle. "You sound so serious. What's the deal? What have I done? Are you going to drag me away in handcuffs and leg shackles?"

Again Allie felt a smidgen of hope. How could Kayla joke around like that if she was truly guilty of giving birth and then tossing her baby in a Dumpster?

"Kayla, we *are* serious," Doug assured her. Allie was surprised by his kind, quiet and collected tone. So far he was handling the situation well. Considering his own emotional investment in the situation, he was handling it *extremely* well. "This is about Jake and what happened the night we found him," he continued.

Kayla was finally silenced. She just sat there and stared at Doug, no nervous smile twitching at her mouth, no fidgeting.

"You know how I've been looking for the person who owned that quilt Jake was found in?" Doug waited for a response, but Kayla said nothing.

"Well, we found out it once belonged to Mary McAllister," he went on, his manner still quiet and calm. "But Liam remembered that he gave it to you, and we figure you must have had that quilt in your possession for the last twenty years. Did we figure right, Kayla?"

Kayla's gaze shifted to Liam, became dreamy, almost glazed. She nodded, a small, wistful smile flitting over her lips. "Yes, Liam gave it to me. He was *nice* to me. I knew I shouldn't, but I took the quilt home and kept it under my bed. I only used it when no one was looking. I didn't want anyone to find out I'd stolen it. I used it just for my most special dolls."

Allie's heart felt like it was breaking in two. *Oh, Kayla! It really was you!*

Doug squatted down in front of Kayla, balancing on the balls of his feet. He looked Kayla directly in the eyes. "Did you wrap Jake in the quilt that night...the night he was born?"

Again Kayla's gaze strayed away from Doug, this time to the window. But it was obvious she wasn't seeing the elm tree outside, or the autumn sunshine dancing off the little red wagon in the yard. She was seeing that night, a month ago, when Jake was born.

"I didn't want him to be cold," she said.

"You mean, when you put him in the Dumpster?" Doug's voice broke on the word "Dumpster."

Kayla's eyes filled with tears. "It was so cold that night. Too cold for a baby to be outside without a blanket. I knew he was better off dead, because God knew *I* couldn't take care of another baby, but it was so *cold*...."

Suddenly she seemed to return to the present and she fixed her tortured gaze on Liam. "I was going to get him out and bring him home. I wasn't sure how I was going to afford to take care of him, or how I could manage if he was half the work Travis is. But I knew I couldn't let him die. He was crying.... He sounded so helpless. Then I saw lights and I heard an engine. I didn't know then, of course, but it was *you*, Liam."

Now the tears were streaming down Kayla's face. Allie cried silent tears, too, and clutched her sister's shaking hands in hers.

"You were really going to get him out of the Dumpster?" Liam asked, and who could blame him if his tone was a little disbelieving.

"Yes, but I got scared when I heard your car. I was covered with blood. I was in terrible pain. I could hardly think. Travis was in the Volvo and I knew he might wake up any moment. I didn't know what to do! I just ran inside the rest room again and locked the door. Then I waited and listened. I figured I still had time to get him out of the Dumpster after you left, Liam."

Allie could imagine the terror, confusion and desperation Kayla was feeling during those moments in the rest room.

"When I realized someone—you, Liam—had found the baby, I was *so* relieved!" Kayla released a long, shuddering sigh. "That's when I knew he'd be okay. In fact, I knew he'd be more than okay because he wouldn't have to have a mother like *me.*"

"Oh, Kayla, you're a wonderful mother to Travis," Allie objected. "And you've taken such good care of Jake, too. I know you must love him."

Kayla shook her head and smiled sadly. "Of course I love him. I couldn't believe it when you brought him by the house that first morning, Allie. I decided that it was just too coincidental that you ended up with him. When you told me how 'right' it felt when you held him, I decided that fate or some higher power must have been involved. You wanted a baby so badly."

"But not *your* baby, Kayla," Allie said.

"I'd buried that night so deep inside me, I really didn't think of Jake as mine," she admitted with that faraway look in her eyes again. Then she focused and turned to Allie. "He's better off with you, sis. As far as I'm concerned, he's *still* yours. You love him like a mother."

Doug stood up and glared down at Kayla, showing his first signs of anger. "But *I'm* his father, Kayla. You had no right to keep your pregnancy from me, and you had no right to throw him away the night he was born. And you sure as hell have no right to give him away now!"

Kayla stared up at Doug, trembling uncontrollably.

"I'm right, aren't I, Kayla?" he persisted. "Jake's *my* baby, isn't he?"

Kayla nodded miserably, then burst into tears. "You didn't love me! You didn't want me! You wanted Allie," she sobbed. "I didn't think you'd want the baby, either."

"You were wrong, Kayla," Doug said sadly, earnestly. He lowered himself to rest on his heels again and reached out to tentatively stroke Kayla's hair. "But I was wrong, too. I've hurt you and used you. And I can't tell you how sorry I am. But I'm going to fix things, Kayla. I promise."

Allie got up and Doug took her place beside Kayla. He put his arm around her and Kayla cried against his shoulder till she was all cried out.

Allie watched and wondered how Doug was going to "fix things," but something inside her knew that somehow he would. This situation seemed to have given him instant maturity. She doubted he'd marry Kayla, because he didn't love her. But she had no doubt that he intended to make sure she didn't do prison time, and that once things were cleared up he'd support her and the baby, both emotionally and financially.

She turned to look at Liam, but caught only a glimpse of the back of him as he walked out the door. The vise around Allie's heart tightened. She wondered if she'd ever see him again.

IN THE NEXT TWO WEEKS, Liam rarely left the boundaries of Mary's property. When he did, it was to take long, solitary hikes in the surrounding mountains or drive through Utah's back country in the Jeep. Then he'd return to the house and chop wood for hours.

Jacob made frequent visits to the house to pick up Mary, or stay and visit with her, and he continued his sessions with Bea. It was through Jacob that Liam heard how Kayla's case was handled and how everyone was dealing with the situation.

Because of Doug's position in the community and his connections in Kamas, he was able to work out a deal with the legal authorities to keep Kayla out of jail. In fact, she was never even charged with any crimes. She was, however, required to get counseling and assigned a caseworker to closely monitor her emotional condition and home environment.

No one could dispute the fact that Kayla was a good mother to Travis, and no one wanted them separated. What her involvement would be in Jake's life was a more complicated issue. Most of them, including Liam, came to believe Kayla's story that she fully intended to retrieve Jake from the Dumpster just before Liam's arrival on the scene. But the fact that she'd tossed him in there in the first place in a moment of desperation warranted a close observation of her mental health and supervision by professionals for a while.

The last Liam heard, Doug and Kayla planned to eventually share custody of Jake, with Kayla's home as primary residence.

Kayla's parents had moved back to Annabella for as long as necessary to help out till she completed her counseling, and for moral support. In the meantime, a woman who lived in Kayla's neighborhood was taking care of Jake until Kayla was deemed by Social Services as capable of doing it herself. She was allowed to visit Jake, and she did regularly.

As for Allie... Liam never asked Jacob how she was doing. He didn't feel he had the right. He would have been glad of news about Allie from Mary, but for some reason his grandmother was keeping mum. Liam could only suppose that Mary thought he didn't deserve news, either, or that it was best that all ties were severed between him and Allie and the whole painful situation put in the past and forgotten.

Liam missed Jake terribly. But he missed Allie more.

Allie. He ached to hold her and comfort her. He could only imagine what she was going through. He told himself that at least she was going to be part of Jake's life as his aunt, but he knew that it would be nothing like being Jake's mom…and Allie would know it, too. And to make matters more painful, Doug was the father.

One wet Friday afternoon Jacob showed up at the house when he wasn't expected by either Mary or Bea. He asked to speak with Liam privately, but promised his "girls" that he wouldn't leave without visiting with them, too.

Liam showed Jacob into the library, motioned him to one of the two plush leather chairs that were pushed up close to the fireplace, then sat down in the other.

Liam was nervous and curious about this private meeting, but he didn't forget to be hospitable. "Can I offer you something, Jacob? A drink, maybe?"

"I've wanted one every day, nearly every hour, for the past two weeks," Jacob said drily. "This business with Kayla has been difficult, to say the least. But I haven't had a drink since I went on that three-month bender after I got back from the war and found out

Mary was married to your grandfather. I don't plan to break my sobriety now. Especially now that—"

Jacob broke off and gave Liam a narrow, questioning look.

"Especially now that Mary's back in your life," Liam finished for him. "Don't worry. I've got nothing against the two of you being together. I just assumed you knew how I felt. But I guess we've never talked about this, have we?"

"I guess we don't need to, if you're okay with it," Jacob said. He paused, considered, then bluntly stated, "If she'll have me, I plan to marry her someday, you know."

Liam was surprised. "No I didn't know. Actually, it never even occurred to me that you'd marry." As soon as the words came out of his mouth, he regretted them. His off-the-cuff comment implied that they were too old for marriage...and everything that went with it.

"Didn't think we old folks still cared about that kind of thing, did you?" Jacob said a little testily. "Well, we *do*. And I intend to make an honest woman out of your grandmother."

Liam felt himself blushing. He was thirty-three years old and he was blushing! Jacob was implying that he and Gran had already— Well, good for them, if that was the case, he decided. At least someone around there was having sex.

Liam smiled. "I think it's great, Jacob. You have my blessing."

Jacob smiled back, but returned to his blunt conversational style immediately. "I didn't come here to talk about Mary, or to ask for your blessing or permission—'' He stopped abruptly, mindful of his manners, and added gruffly, ''Although it *is* appreciated. I came to talk about Bea.''

Liam was all attention. ''So, you're finally ready to talk about her! I suppose this means she doesn't need you anymore.''

Jacob bobbed his head. ''You're right. She hasn't needed me as a doctor for some time. We've talked our insides out and she's got a whole lot of things off her chest.'' He paused, pursed his lips, then added, ''Now maybe you should get a few things off *your* chest.''

Liam shifted uncomfortably. ''If you're referring to my secret plans to adopt Jake, I've already—''

''No, I'm referring to the same tragedy that's depressed Bea for so long. I'm talking about the death of your wife and son. You haven't dealt with it, Liam.''

Liam was instantly defensive. ''How the hell could you know that? Besides, my feelings are private and none of your business.''

''Were they none of Bea's business, either?''

Liam stood up abruptly and paced the carpet. ''I asked you to help Bea, Jacob. And you did. I'm grateful, but that doesn't give you the right to try to analyze me.''

''Liam, you kept your grief to yourself, and in the process you taught Bea to keep her grief bottled up, too.''

Liam sat down again. ''Are you trying to tell me

I'm the reason Bea's been sick and unhappy for the past year?''

"Not entirely and not intentionally. She was probably born and raised with the same tendency toward a 'stiff upper lip' as you were.''

"But I *tried* to get her to talk about her feelings,'' Liam protested.

"But did you talk to her about *your* feelings? Your sadness about your wife's death?''

Liam was dumbfounded. Jacob was right! He'd never shared his feelings with Bea, or with anyone else for that matter. "She was trying to be like me,'' Liam said dully. "Poor Bea.''

Jacob said nothing more, just let his theory sink in. Liam resolved then and there to be more emotionally open with Bea. And to talk to someone when *he* needed to talk, too.

"I *have* felt better lately,'' Liam finally offered. "Despite bottling it up.''

"I know,'' Jacob agreed. "You've been mending despite yourself. Bea just needed a little more help. But don't beat yourself up, Liam. You're a good father.''

"Does it ever get easier?'' Liam asked wryly.

"No,'' was Jacob's blunt reply. Then he slapped his knees and stood up. "My work is done—if you can call something I enjoy doing so much 'work'—but I hope you don't mind if I still keep company with Bea now and then. She's a sweet little girl and she and Mary and I have some good times together.''

Liam stood up, too. "For as long as we're here.''

Jacob gave Liam another of his keen-eyed looks. "You're thinking of leaving soon, are you?"

"Our home is in England, Jacob. We've already stayed longer than we intended. I had hoped to take Mary back with us to stay through the holidays, which is what she normally does, but I suppose she's going to be staying in Utah this year?" He ended the sentence with a question mark in his voice.

Jacob dug his hands into his back trouser pockets. "I know Mary's got a bunch of grandkids over there, and I know they want to see her and she wants to see them. If she wants to go to England, she can go. I don't mind. Maybe I'll even offer to go with her?" Now Jacob's voice held a question mark.

Liam wasn't sure how to reply. He didn't know what his relatives would think of this Yank making claims on their beloved Mum and Gran and Auntie Mary. But there was only one way to find out.

"Go for it, Jacob," Liam advised him with a grin. "I'll put in a good word for you."

"I just might," Jacob replied, thrusting his chin out. "I wouldn't mind seeing England. Never made a trip over there, you know, but I've thought about it a lot over the years."

Liam chuckled. "I'll just bet you have."

He sobered quickly, however, when he thought about Allie spending her Christmas alone. Jacob was turning to leave the room and search out Mary and Bea, but Liam detained him with a touch on the arm and a question that seemed to burst from his lips accidentally. "But what about Allie?"

Jacob looked over his shoulder, his expression

shrewd and guarded. "It's about time you asked. What *about* Allie?"

Liam felt awkward, to say the least. "If you go to England, won't she be spending Christmas alone? Considering everything, I think that would be pretty hard on her."

"Her parents will still be in town at Christmastime," Jacob assured him. "Allie won't be alone."

Liam still wasn't satisfied. Maybe that's exactly what he was afraid of...that Allie wouldn't be alone. He thought of Doug and wondered if the sheriff of Annabella still intended to pursue Allie despite everything that had happened. And he couldn't help but wonder if Allie would be more likely to go back to Doug now that Jake was a permanent fixture in her ex-husband's life.

"I know what you're thinking, Liam, and it's not going to happen."

Liam had been caught brooding, and he wondered if he'd been caught "thinking," too. It certainly felt as though Jacob had just read his mind! He said nothing and waited...hopefully.

Jacob released a long hiss of breath. "She's not going to go back to Doug. And if you had half the brain God gave a goat, you'd know that, McAllister. She's not in love with *him*."

Liam overlooked the goat comparison and zeroed in on the emphasis Jacob had placed on that last word. She's not in love with *him*. So, was it possible that she was in love with...well...*him?* Liam figured she was still angry with him. He thought she might even hate him for his deceitfulness.

Liam opened his mouth, but Jacob raised his hand and waved it in a gesture of dismissal. "I've said all I'm going to say. The rest is up to you."

After Jacob left, Liam stood for a long time in the middle of the library, wondering just what the old guy had meant by "the rest." Then he considered what he, Liam, wanted "the rest" to mean. The rest of his life? The rest of Allie's life? The rest of *their* life together?

Liam sat down as the reality of what he was feeling, thinking and hoping rolled over him like an avalanche. He was in love with Allie Lockwood. Their lives were oceans apart. But somehow he had to make it work.

He checked his watch. It was five-thirty on a very rainy November afternoon. He wondered what Allie was doing. He wondered if she was okay.

Chapter Thirteen

Allie had her head in the oven when the doorbell rang. She sat back on her heels and debated whether or not to answer it. She couldn't think of a single person she felt like seeing right now. Nor did she want anyone seeing *her* in her present state, either. She started to put her head back in the oven, but the doorbell rang again, followed by three knocks.

Allie struggled to her feet, her aching back reminding her of all the getting up and down she'd already done that day, threw down the grimy sponge she'd been using on the inside of her non-self-cleaning oven, and started down the hall. She was a doctor and it might be an emergency, after all, and she did care about her patients and had a responsibility to them. She thought wearily that she'd probably never have the luxury of ignoring the doorbell *or* the telephone.

Just before grabbing the knob to open the door, she wiped her moist palms against her jean-covered bottom and pushed back a dangly strand of hair. She was sure she was going to scare whoever was at the door with her dirty and disheveled appearance, but she had the cleanest house this side of the Mississippi…except for her oven, and that was going to be spotless, too, even if it killed her. Cleaning had always been therapeutic for her, and boy did she ever need therapy these days.

When Allie carelessly opened the front door, the last person on earth she'd expected to see again was standing on her porch. It was a wet November day that was fast becoming night, with a frigid wind stripping the last withered leaves off the trees...and Liam McAllister was not wearing a coat. He looked gorgeous in his hunter-green, crew-neck sweater and jeans, but he also looked cold and would soon be soaked if he didn't get under a roof as soon as possible. Instinctively, without thinking about the consequences, she did the human thing. She stepped aside and motioned him in.

"Thank you," Liam said, rubbing his arms as he stood hesitantly just inside her door. "It's not a good day to be outside."

Allie stared at him for a moment, flustered and embarrassed, then realized as a blast of icy wind cut right through her oversize T-shirt that she'd left the door open, and shut it.

Now the full impact of the situation hit her. Liam McAllister, all fresh and clean and handsome, with beads of rain melting in his glossy chestnut-brown hair, was standing in her immaculate living room where the only thing out of place was *her*.

Despite a blush that crept up her neck and suffused her cheeks with heat and, no doubt, quite a lot of color, she had the presence of mind to wonder what the heck he was doing there. He'd done another one of his disappearing acts after they'd confronted Kayla at her house two weeks ago, so Allie figured he meant to stay away permanently. She'd thought about it a lot, and she was never sure whether or not she was glad he'd kept his distance. She still wasn't sure....

"You're surprised to see me," he said, finally breaking the awkward silence between them.

"Well, I wasn't exactly expecting company," she replied. *And certainly not you,* she added to herself. She gestured helplessly at her work clothes, un-made-up face and straggly hair. "I've...I've been cleaning the oven. And everything else in the house, too," she finished lamely.

Liam nodded and made a polite show of looking around the room, then remarked, "I can see that. Everything is very...er...neat and tidy."

"And I look like the Wreck of the Hesperas," Allie said bluntly. Avoiding direct eye contact with Liam, she self-consciously ran a hand through her hair, trying to arrange it into some semblance of order. Then she remembered the night they'd made love.... He'd suggested then that she comb her hair with her fingers before answering the door. That night Doug had been standing on the porch and that was the beginning of the end of her "fling" with Liam.

"I think you look...well...*cute,*" Liam said.

Allie met his gaze and was disarmed by the warm twinkle in his green eyes. Her heart fluttered and she couldn't help a small, wry smile. "Good try, Liam. I know I'm a mess, but it's gallant of you to lie."

He'd started to smile, too, but when the word "lie" ended her sentence, his smile faded away. They'd made love, then parted ways immediately afterward because she'd discovered his deceitful activities regarding Jake.

"Allie, can we talk? You not only didn't expect to see me today, but you probably didn't want to see me ever again. But I have some things to say and I only hope you'll permit me to—"

"Yes, Liam," she interrupted him. "We can talk. But why don't you sit down for a minute while I go clean up? I feel at a decided disadvantage looking like a chimney sweep from a Dickens novel."

Liam released a huff of breath, as if he'd been holding it forever, then nodded his assent. "I'll be happy to sit and wait. I'll even wait till you take a bath, if you want."

Yet another reminder of the night they'd made love, Allie thought distractedly. He'd waited while she took a bath that night, too. Was he making these comparisons on purpose?

"No, I'll just wash my hands and face," Allie assured him with more firmness than necessary. "I'll just be a jiff."

Allie quickly went to her bedroom and shut the door. She went immediately into the adjoining bathroom and was horrified when she looked in the mirror for the first time since she got up that morning. It was worse than she thought! She had dirt smears on her face, cobwebs in her hair from carting off clutter to store in the attic, bloodshot eyes from the flying dust at the mercy of her cleaning rag, and not a stitch of makeup on to offset the damage.

Maybe she didn't have time for a bath, but she was going to break the world's record at taking a shower.

She threw off her clothes, soaped up furiously, got out, put on a clean pair of jeans and a flannel shirt, ran a comb through her wet hair, slashed on some lipstick, dabbed on some mascara, and felt marginally better. One last glance in the mirror told her she still wouldn't win any beauty contests today, but at least she was respectable-looking and clean.

She'd been so busy worrying about her appearance, she hadn't thought at length about why Liam was there and what he might want to talk about. Now that she was walking down the hall toward the living room, toward *Liam,* she thought about it. He was probably on his way back to England in the morning, she decided, and had simply come to make one last apology and tell her he hoped she had a very nice life, yada yada yada. Not exactly a fairy tale ending, but life wasn't a fairy tale, was it? She'd known that for a long time, so why was she so painfully disappointed?

When she entered the room, Liam was looking out the front window where an eerie, golden twilight was peeking around the dark edges of wind-driven storm clouds. He turned and his gaze traveled the length of her. She could actually *feel* every second his eyes were on her. "Ah, you took a bath anyway," he said with a smile.

"No, just a shower," she assured him, not wanting him to think she'd gone to any trouble. "I felt like Pig Pen, with my own little cloud of dirt following me around."

She sat down, and he followed suit. She was on the couch and he was on the chair furthest away from the couch. "Why the cleaning frenzy?" he asked conversationally.

"Well, with my folks in town, we're having Thanksgiving this year at my house." It was true, but that wasn't why she'd been cleaning.

"Thanksgiving isn't for another three weeks," Liam pointed out. "You sure don't let things wait till the last minute, do you?"

Allie couldn't stand it anymore. "We're beating around the bush here, Liam. You didn't come to make small talk with me, and I'm not in the mood anyway. Let me get the ball rolling.... I have been cleaning like a maniac in a fierce attempt to get my mind off things that are painful to think about. I have been cleaning for therapy. I have been cleaning to *forget.*"

Liam's immediate expression of sympathy was very nearly Allie's undoing. She could handle anything but sympathy. But she fought back the tears and held her head up.

"I was wondering how you were coping," he admitted. "I like to do physical things, too, when I'm stressed or sad. I've been hiking and chopping wood like a mad man."

"Because you're...sad?" she asked hesitantly. "Sad about Jake?"

"Hell, Allie," Liam confessed, leaning forward, his forearms on his thighs and his hands clasped. "I'm sad about a lot of things. I miss Jake. But I'm mad at myself for trying to steal him from you and hurting you in the process. I'm sad that you don't trust me anymore. But I understand."

She looked down, the tears building. She fought them. She gulped back the ache in her throat.

But Liam just seemed to be warming to his topic. "I'm sad about Kayla. I'm sorry she was brought to such a point of desperation in her life without anyone suspecting. But she was very good at hiding her misery under a facade of fake cheer and it was nobody's fault that she got to that desperate point."

Now the tears spilled over and silently slid down Allie's cheeks.

"I'm sad that my wife died and I didn't have the guts to outwardly express my grief, to allow my daughter and others to see my grief, thereby giving Bea permission to grieve, too."

Allie sniffed and wiped her face with the back of her hand. Suddenly Liam was beside her on the sofa and a snowy white handkerchief appeared under her nose. She took it and blew.

"Now it's your turn, Allie," Liam said gently, his voice so near her ear she could feel the faint stirring of his breath. She got a chill down her back. "Tell me what you're sad about. Believe me, sharing your feelings is even better than cleaning the oven."

"I don't want to," she mumbled, feeling like a stubborn child, but not caring. "I'm tired of sadness. I want to be happy."

"I'll make a deal with you then," he offered. "After you tell me why you're sad, you can tell me why you're happy, too. And don't tell me you have nothing to be happy about."

She looked up at him through her wet lashes.

"Well, if you think it's so easy to come up with as much happy as sad, you start," she dared him.

"Okay," he said, seeming to actually welcome the challenge.

He sat back in the sofa and trained his eyes on the ceiling. She stared at his chiseled profile, the firm chin, the strong neck.

"I'm happy that Kayla is getting the help she needs. I'm happy that she didn't have to go to jail and Travis still has his mom. I'm happy that Jake's still in your life, even if it's not exactly turning out the way you planned. I'm happy that Bea's healthy again and that her recovery—thanks to your grandfather—taught me things about myself that might make my life a little easier in the future. I'm happy that Mary and Jacob are happy, and that they found each other again after all these years."

She continued to stare at him. Was he through? But he hadn't said a word about *her*. Then he shifted his gaze from the ceiling and looked sideways at Allie. She loved the feel of his eyes on her almost as much as she loved the feel of his hands and lips and… Oops, she was getting carried away.

"I'm happy that you let me in tonight, Allie," he continued, his deep, gentle voice mesmerizing. "I'm happy that you're still listening to me and haven't booted me out the door. I'm happy that Jacob made me realize that I could grieve for Victoria without bitterness and get on with my life. I'm happy I realized that it wasn't just Jake that gave me a new lease on life this fall, but it was also you."

Startled, she looked away. He sat forward and covered her hand with his. Oh, how she loved his touch! "It was really more *you* than Jake, Allie. I might have saved his life, but you saved *mine*. You made me feel alive again, Allie, and I'll always be grateful."

She swallowed and swallowed, forcing back the emotion. She didn't know what to say. She still didn't know if he was trying to tell her he cared about her, or reciting a goodbye speech, or both.

"Now it's your turn," he said, squeezing the hand he still held captive.

"I'm sad and happy about the same things you are, Liam," she said in a small voice, her gaze fixed on the carpet in front of her bare feet. "Jake, Kayla, Travis, Doug, Gramps and Mary." She smiled. "Busy Bea."

"Go on," he urged her in a low, persuasive voice.

"But there are some additional things I should probably mention. I'm...I'm happy you're *here*," she said, returning the hand squeeze. "I'm happy I realized— weeks ago—that you really did plan to call off the adoption, and I'm happy I forgave you for...that whole thing. I'm sad I didn't tell you this sooner."

She turned and looked him bravely in the eyes. "I'm happy we made love that night. I'll never regret it. And, lastly, I'm sad you're going back to England."

Liam cupped her chin in his free hand, his index finger stroking her cheek. "I'm happy to tell you, Allie, that I have no intention of going back to England till Christmastime. And that if you're interested in not regretting making love to me again, we'll have lots of time and opportunity between now and December twenty-fifth."

Allie's tears started flowing again, and Liam kissed them away. He caught her against his chest and held her close, murmuring endearments. As this went on for several blissful minutes, Allie thought she'd died and gone to heaven. One minute she was cleaning the oven and the next minute she was melting in the arms of the man she loved.

If only she'd been brave enough to tell him *that*...

"I have one more thing to tell you, Allie," Liam whispered hoarsely, pulling back and smiling into her flushed face. "It's something that makes me really happy. I'm not sure you're ready to hear this, but— forgive me again—I can't seem to wait any longer."

Allie's heart skittered and skipped. She was imagining all kinds of things. Everything but what she heard him say.

"I love you, Allie. And despite the fact that we live on different continents, I want us to find a way to be together. I want to marry you, Allie."

Swooning was generally thought to be confined to the parlors of frail Victorian women in tight corsets, but Allie was on the verge of stealing their signature shtick. "Wh...what did you say?"

"I said I love you," Liam repeated patiently, then nibbled her ear. "I want to marry you. Do you want me to say it again?"

"No, I—"

"Because I will if you want me to." He drew back suddenly. "But maybe I'm going too fast. I'll shut up if you want me to. I can be patient. But I promise you, Allie, I'm going to work on you like a tick on a dog till you say yes. Yes, you love me. Yes, you'll marry me.''

She couldn't help it. Despite her flustered state, she laughed. "Like a tick on a dog? Where did you pick up that lovely expression?''

"From your grandfather," he admitted sheepishly. "It's a common American expression, isn't it?''

"Well, I wouldn't call it exactly common. And I'm not sure it works in the context you used it.''

"But am I getting my point across anyway?'' Liam asked, laughing along with her.

Allie saw the anxiety in Liam's eyes even as he joked around with her. He was waiting for a response to his declaration of love and proposal of marriage. Her admission of equal feelings of love and a ready "yes" to his proposal was on the tip of her tongue. But then she remembered. He didn't know about her infertility.

"What is it, Allie?'' He'd obviously seen the stricken look come into her eyes at the exact moment she remembered why she had no right to marry Liam McAllister. The words he'd spoken that first night he'd kissed her came back to her, clear as a bell. *"I want to marry again. I want a family. I want more children. Several. You can't imagine how wonderful it's been holding Jake and experiencing those feelings of a new father again.''*

"Liam, I can't marry you," she said miserably, her eyes filling with tears again.

"Because you don't love me?'' he asked her.

"No, because I can't have children," she blurted out. She saw no reason to make up some other excuse for fear he'd be noble and stick by his proposal. She'd see through that in a New York minute. She wanted only honesty between them now, and knew that's what Liam wanted, too.

She watched for the shock and disappointment to show on his handsome face, obliterating the happy glow of the last few minutes. But he didn't look shocked or disappointed. He didn't even look mildly surprised.

"You knew already?" she said, her voice rising to an adolescent squeak.

"Of course I knew," he replied, an unmistakable note of relief in his voice. "I was afraid you were refusing me because you didn't love me, couldn't imagine us ever making a life together."

"But you didn't know the night we made love," she said, still needing reassurance.

"No, but I've known ever since then. Gran told me."

She nodded. "I see. Yes, everyone seemed to know but you, Liam. Were you surprised?"

He stroked her face and smiled wistfully. "Yes, a little. And sorry for your sake that you couldn't have babies, Allie. Now I'm sorry for my sake, too, because I'm sure a combination of you and me would have been delightful. We'd have made a child that would alternately overwhelm us with pride and love, then have us pulling our hair out in fistfuls."

Allie laughed softly, sadly.

Liam pulled her into his arms. "But we can adopt as many children as we want, love. We already know that we're both perfectly capable of loving a child distractedly, whether or not he or she is biologically ours.''

She knew he was right. And that meant there was only one possible response to his declaration of love and proposal of marriage.

''I love you, Liam McAllister, despite the fact that you're rich and famous and titled,'' she whispered in his ear. ''And I want to marry you even though the paparazzi will find me one day in a flannel shirt, shopping at Safeway, and splash the unflattering image all over the front of their rag sheet.''

She was teasing, but he held her closer and whispered protectively, ''I'll try to protect you from the publicity, Allie, but I won't lie to you. Reporters will follow us around for a while, especially in England.''

''We're going to live in England, then?'' she asked, pulling back and smiling at him coyly. ''What about the good old U.S. of A?''

''We have to live in England at least part of the year,'' Liam answered reasonably, ''but I'm sure we can work out the details to satisfy both of us.''

''Yes, I'm sure we can,'' she agreed, as content as a kitten and as sure of her happiness as someone with a crystal ball.

''But back to the paparazzi... Eventually the novelty will wear off...I hope. And we'll just be another married couple not worth a snapshot. Sound good to you?''

''Liam,'' Allie answered earnestly, happily. ''It sounds like a dream come true.''

Epilogue

Three months later, at Mary's "little cabin in Utah"...

"We have to *go*, Daddy."

Liam turned from the full-length mirror where he was fiddling with his bow tie and saw Bea standing just inside the room, her hand on the doorknob and an urgent look on her face.

Liam smiled. "We've got plenty of time, Busy Bea. What's your hurry?"

Bea came in, the full skirt of her pale-pink dress, and all the petticoats underneath, rustling as she walked, her patent leather shoes clip-clopping on the hardwood floor. "The wedding can't start without us," she argued. "And I just *don't* want to be late."

He bent down and tapped her on the nose. "Neither do I, love. And we won't be, I promise. By the way, did I tell you that you're the prettiest flower girl I've ever seen?"

This finally got a smile out of her. "Yes, Daddy. About a million times."

Liam feigned surprise. "I have? Well, it's the

truth." He turned back to the mirror and surveyed himself from top to toe, all decked out in a black tuxedo with a creamy rose in his lapel. "How do I look, Bea? The monkey suit is okay, but I can't seem to get this tie just right...."

Liam heard the scrape of a chair being dragged across the floor and he turned to see Bea climbing on top of it. "Come here," she ordered, then motioned him over with a couple of waggles of her index finger.

Amused, he obeyed. "You're going to fix it for me, are you?"

With Bea standing on the chair they were almost, but not quite, eye to eye. Liam watched her fondly as she concentrated on her job, then patted the tie with her small palm when she was through. "There," she said with satisfaction. "Much better. Turn around and look, Daddy."

Once again, Liam obeyed his daughter and turned to look in the mirror. She was right, the tie was much straighter. He looked at her in the mirror, at her small, heart-shaped face peeking around from behind him. "How'd you learn to do that, Busy Bea?"

She rested her cheek against his shoulder and hugged his arm. "I used to watch Mummy do it," she said simply.

Liam's heart swelled with love. "You're a lot like your mum, you know."

"I know," she answered seriously. "I think this is a bea-*U*-tiful wedding, and she would, too. And she'd think Allie was right about the cream roses going better with everything, even though this *is* Valentine's Day and some people will wonder why we didn't use pink or red."

"Well, I've always thought Allie had very good taste," Liam agreed. "She picked me, didn't she?"

Bea giggled. "Daddy!" But when her dimpled smile vanished and she looked suddenly thoughtful, Liam turned to face her.

He slipped his large hands around her small waist, which was circled in satin with a big bow in the back. "What's the matter, Bea? What are you thinking?"

"I'm thinking about that first night when we came to see Gran, and we found Jake in the rubbish bin."

"Yes?"

"And how I told you I thought God sent the baby because we'd lost ours?"

Memories of that night still brought back painful feelings. "Yes, I remember," he said finally, wondering where this was leading to. A few months ago he might have tried to change the subject, but he'd learned from both Dr. Lockwoods that it was better to talk about your feelings and not bottle them up.

"Well, I still think God wanted us to find Jake, Daddy, but not because he was supposed to be ours. I think it was God's way of helping us find Allie. And look at all the good things that have happened since then."

Liam drew Bea to his chest and hugged her. "You are *so* smart, Bea. How'd you get so smart?"

"*Mum* was smart," she offered as an answer to such a mystery.

Liam laughed. "Oh, so you got your beauty *and* your brains from your mum, eh? I don't suppose you got anything good from your dear old dad?"

He tickled her and she giggled and squealed.

Suddenly the door swung open and Allie sashayed

in, flung out her arm and announced, "Here comes the bride!"

Liam and Bea both turned and smiled expectantly as Mary followed Allie into the room. His diminutive grandmother looked elegant and feminine in a cream-colored, beautifully tailored suit with matching pumps, and a hat the Queen Mum would have died for. Her delicate cheeks pinkened as they all three looked her over.

"Oh, Gran," said Bea, as Liam lifted her down from the chair. "You look bea-*U*-tiful!"

"Doesn't she?" Allie agreed. "Gramps' eyes are gonna pop out when he sees her."

Bea giggled, no doubt envisioning Dr. Jake's eyeballs rolling down the aisle at the old Annabella church on Center Street, and everyone chasing them.

"I know it's probably foolish," Mary said, self-consciously smoothing her trim skirt. "But, you know, I really *do* feel like a blushing bride! I never thought I'd be lucky enough to have two wonderful marriages in my lifetime."

So far, Liam had said nothing. Now Mary looked at him with a question in her eyes. Liam was sure she was thinking that he had been okay so far about her renewed romance with Jacob, but today—her wedding day—was the real test.

"Gran, you look beautiful and happy," he said, crossing the room to give her a hug. And while he still held her close, he whispered, "Grandfather would want you to be happy. And I don't think he'd mind that Jacob was the reason." He squeezed her and chuckled. "Well, not *much*."

When they separated, Gran's eyes were shiny with tears. "I won't be a watering pot at my own wedding and walk down the aisle with a red nose," she declared, lifting her chin determinedly. "So there'll be no more sentimental claptrap, and, besides, it's time to go! We don't want to be late. It's very ill-mannered to be late to your own wedding."

"That's what I told Daddy," Bea said, rolling her eyes. She took her grandmother by the hand. "Come on, Gran, let's go get our coats."

Allie and Liam exchanged amused glances which blossomed into full-blown smiles as they eyed each other appreciatively. "You look very James Bond in that tuxedo," Allie said, sidling over with a coy gleam in her eyes. Liam liked her dress. It was a simple, pale-pink sheath that skimmed her trim figure to perfection…and his distraction.

"And you look like you could stir a martini with the best of 'em," he murmured as he pulled her into his arms.

"I can stir up just about anything with the best of 'em," she assured him. She clasped her hands behind his neck and let her head fall back till her blond hair skimmed her shoulders. She was growing it longer for him. She smiled up at him and he contemplated her mouth hungrily.

"I don't suppose you'd let me kiss you right now, darling? I'd smear your lipstick for sure."

"Lipstick can easily be reapplied. That's why I carry an extra tube in my purse, for just such occasions when I find my husband too irresistible to resist."

He pulled her closer, her lips an inch away. "I hope you'll always find me irresistible, Allie, my darling wife."

"I think it's a safe bet that I always *shall,* my

lord,'' she teased, ''as long as you never lose that sexy accent.''

''Don't worry. If it starts slipping, I'll watch a few David Niven movies and practice...practice... practice.''

Each ''practice'' brought his mouth closer to hers. Finally they were kissing. As always, it was wonderful, tender, sensual. He never got tired of making love to his passionate American wife. Ah, if only they *could* make love....

''Ahem!''

Liam and Allie broke apart and focused their dazed gazes on the door. Ribchester stood there, dressed for the wedding in an old-fashioned coat with a tail and wearing a top hat with a cream-colored band around its crown.

''You look dapper, Ribchester,'' Liam told him. ''But *I* have to walk the bride down the aisle. You might have spared me the embarrassment of outshining me, you know.''

''Hurumph,'' was Ribchester's dignified reply to this raillery, but he had to suppress a grin.

''I suppose you've come to tell me that the car is waiting.''

''Indeed, my lord, that is exactly what I've come to tell you. And that your relatives from England did not come all the way to Utah to be kept waiting in the church while you...er...dallied.''

''And the bride's getting a bit twitchy,'' came Mrs. Preedy's voice as she hurried down the hall. Liam saw her whiz past, a blur of black silk and a black, pillbox hat decorated for the occasion with real roses. Mrs. Preedy wore her black silk to every special occasion, be it a wedding, christening or funeral. He had been well acquainted with it for many years.

"We'll be right there, Ribchester," Liam assured him. "Go along with your wife now."

Ribchester gave him one of his looks—one hoary brow haughtily raised over a steely gleam of eyes. It meant, "You'd better be." It was a look as familiar to Liam as Mrs. Preedy's black silk dress and pillbox hat.

Ribchester departed and Allie cozied up to his chest again, the feel of her soft curves against him intoxicating.

"I guess we'd better go," she murmured reluctantly, a sleepy sexy smile curving her lips.

"There's always tonight, darling," he promised her, exercising all his willpower as he extricated himself from her embrace and walked her toward the door.

"If I don't fall asleep from exhaustion," she warned him.

He cocked a brow. "You know you won't."

She grinned. "You're right. I won't."

They were in the hall and he was helping her slip into her coat. She turned and said, "Speaking of sleep, did I tell you about the dream I had last night?"

"No, darling, why don't you tell me about it…on the way to the car?"

"Well, it was about a baby. She had beautiful olive skin and dark, dark eyes. They turned up at the corners.… Very exotic. What do you think it means?"

Liam smiled to himself. He knew exactly what it meant. It meant another of Allie's dreams was about to come true.

IT WAS a bea-*U*-tiful wedding, and besides all Mary's relatives from England, most of the townspeople of

Annabella squeezed into the church to see Doctor Jacob Lockwood and Mary Hayes McAllister exchange vows. Many commented that "it was about time," and no one threw rocks at the bride.

It had been a thrill for Mary to become reacquainted with old friends, and make new ones, too, as she ventured out more and more with Jacob during their "very proper" four-month courtship. While some folks might have resented Mary when Jacob first returned from the war to find out his fiancée had lost her heart to another, years of watching Jacob enjoy a loving marriage to Althea Rutherford, a hometown favorite, made them willing to give Mary a little slack...as the Americans say.

Some of the ladies of Annabella even went so far as to admit that *they* might have been tempted to fall into the arms of Cecil McAllister, too, if he was half as handsome and charming as his grandson.

The wedding party was small. Liam gave away the bride, but there were too many people on both sides of the family to choose from in the Best Man and Maid of Honor category, so Mary and Jacob settled for a flower girl and a ring bearer. Bea flung flowers beautifully and Travis carried the rings all the way up the aisle before finally dropping them at Jacob's feet. This drew an indulgent chuckle from the congregation and a wide, sheepish grin from Travis.

Jacob tousled Travis's hair and sent him to his mother, who was sitting on the third row on the groom's side with little Jake, gurgling and happy, propped in her lap and Doug seated at her side. Doug and Kayla had developed a warm friendship as they oversaw the rearing of their son, and Doug had be-

come a surrogate father to Travis, as well, which did
a great deal to calm the boy down. Kayla's counseling
was giving her the self-confidence she'd sorely needed
for most of her life, and Doug's financial and emotional support was eliminating a lot of her stress.

There was talk about town that maybe, just *maybe,*
Sheriff Doug Renshaw was ready to settle down. He
didn't seem to mind Allie's marriage back in December. And he looked downright happy at Jacob's nuptials. So it seemed entirely feasible that he might be
contemplating his own future. Time would tell.

Liam had fast become a favorite about town. Who
couldn't like someone so unremittingly cheerful, and
with not a bit of the high and mighty about him, despite his money and titles? And who, knowing his
tragic past, couldn't be happy he'd found love and a
new lease on life with Allie Lockwood, who'd certainly had her own fair share of troubles?

It just seemed so romantic that a Yank grandfather
and his granddaughter had found their perfect fit with
a Brit grandmother and her grandson. And it was a
great story to tell visiting relatives, and anyone else
who would listen.

The best, the most romantic part of the story, was
when Liam whisked Allie away for Christmas to his
big Victorian mansion in Bridekirk where she met
most of his English relatives in one fell swoop. It
didn't take much after that for Liam to convince her
to marry him on Christmas Eve in the family chapel,
right there on the grounds of his estate.

At first the townspeople weren't sure what to call
the new viscountess when she returned from the holidays with her new husband and daughter. But when
it was widely reported that she was seen in the check-

out line at Safeway having a good laugh at her own picture in the latest *National Intruder,* everyone knew she was still just "Allie."

All through a snowy January, Liam and Bea had stayed on in Annabella, living in Allie's house and helping Mary and Jacob plan their wedding. But not without the paparazzi....

Once they realized that Liam had pulled off a courtship and wedding completely without their knowledge, thereby eliminating the usual hovering helicopters at their nuptials, reporters determinedly followed the newlyweds to Utah.

The tabloids offered top dollar for the first pictures that could be got of the new Lady Roderick, and flights to Salt Lake City were soon booked. Several reporters got lost en route to Annabella, and some, seeing the snowy peaks of the Wasatch mountains, were tempted away to ski at the expense of their unsuspecting editors. But despite the casualties, several paparazzi made it to Annabella and established a stakeout in front of Allie's home and office, only leaving their posts to drink coffee, eat pie, and generally loiter at Bill and Nada's Diner.

Imagine the reporters' delight when Allie and Liam showed no inclination to hide from the cameras! They even allowed pictures of Bea whenever the three of them ventured out to run errands, build snowmen, and shovel the walks.

Within a week, however, the British and American tabloids had enough pictures of Liam and his new bride to paper their office walls, thus greatly diminishing their value. Plus, although the story was quaint and novel and sweet, there appeared to be nothing scandalous going on, and making up something news-worthy seemed hardly worth the trouble.

Not even the distance between their native countries seemed to be putting a hitch in the bliss of the newly married couple. They'd decided that Allie would pass on her practice to her brother, Tom, who was a doctor in Salt Lake and had been pining to return to Anna-bella, but knew the small town didn't need and couldn't support two doctors. Now he could move back and take over and Allie wouldn't be leaving her patients in the lurch. All this was scheduled to happen in the summer, when it would be easier to switch Tom's small children to their new school.

Allie was going to open a practice in Bridekirk, a growing town that needed a doctor, and she was look-ing forward to the challenge.

All their holidays would be spent in Utah with Mary and Jacob at the cabin. The large house was going to be greatly utilized now that Mary's relatives from En-gland had discovered the rustic charm of Utah and were promising to revisit, not to mention Jacob's fam-ily and many mutual friends just itching to pay a call. Cecil had been right to build such a large house, after all.

So, within a month, the only reporter seen at Bill and Nada's Diner was Vivien DeSpain, who wrote garden party reviews for the *Annabella Gazette* and took pictures of potted geraniums. By Valentine's Day Annabella had settled back into its usual small-town rhythm, just as Liam predicted it would.

There was *one* bit of excitement after Jacob and Mary tied the knot, however. On a snowy afternoon late in February, a sedan pulled up in front of Allie's house. Allie watched as a woman stepped out, re-

trieved a small bundle from the back seat, and walked
carefully with it to her front door.

"Right on time," Liam said, startling Allie as he
seemed to have snuck up behind her from somewhere
in the house.

"Who is it? And what has she got?" Allie wanted
to know.

"You'll see," chirped Bea, running to open the
door.

"Hello, Mr. McAllister," the woman said, as she
stepped inside.

"Hello, Mrs. Rampton," Liam replied, obviously
well acquainted with the woman. "How was your
drive from Salt Lake?"

Who *was* this woman? Allie wondered, as she
looked from Liam's inscrutable face to Bea's sup-
pressed glee.

"Good. It's only snowing a little and the roads were
fine. It's a bit nippy out, though, but don't worry, we
bundled up warm."

We? thought Allie. What *we?* But then she saw.
Mrs. Rampton was holding…a baby.

Allie's heart started beating like a bunny's. Way too
fast and jumping all over the place. Was it possible?
Had Liam made arrangements to adopt a baby without
telling her? As a rule, she didn't like surprises, but this
would be the best surprise of her life.

"Breathe, Allie," Liam advised her, rubbing her
back with his hand.

Allie didn't realize she'd been holding her breath.
And she didn't realize she'd started crying till she
tasted the tears on her lips.

"Would you like to hold her, Mrs. McAllister?"
Her?

Allie watched as Mrs. Rampton pulled back the blanket and revealed the baby's face. She had olive skin and dark, dark eyes. Exotic eyes, tilted up at the corners.

"We got her from China!" Bea exclaimed excitedly, no longer able to hold back the glee.

"And I'd made the arrangements before you told me about your dream, Allie," Liam whispered, then gave her a little push forward. "Now go hold your baby."

Allie looked at Liam, her heart too full for words. Oh, how she loved him! His eyes told her he loved her back, but she already knew that.

Allie held out her arms…and Mrs. Rampton filled them with a dream come true.

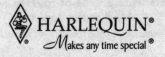

Princes...Princesses...
London Castles...New York Mansions...
To live the life of a royal!

In 2002, Harlequin Books lets you escape to a world of royalty with these royally themed titles:

Temptation:
January 2002—*A Prince of a Guy* (#861)
February 2002—*A Noble Pursuit* (#865)

American Romance:
The Carradignes: American Royalty (Editorially linked series)
March 2002—*The Improperly Pregnant Princess* (#913)
April 2002—*The Unlawfully Wedded Princess* (#917)
May 2002—*The Simply Scandalous Princess* (#921)
November 2002—*The Inconveniently Engaged Prince* (#945)

Intrigue:
The Carradignes: A Royal Mystery (Editorially linked series)
June 2002—*The Duke's Covert Mission* (#666)

Chicago Confidential
September 2002—*Prince Under Cover* (#678)

The Crown Affair
October 2002—*Royal Target* (#682)
November 2002—*Royal Ransom* (#686)
December 2002—*Royal Pursuit* (#690)

Harlequin Romance:
June 2002—*His Majesty's Marriage* (#3703)
July 2002—*The Prince's Proposal* (#3709)

Harlequin Presents:
August 2002—*Society Weddings* (#2268)
September 2002—*The Prince's Pleasure* (#2274)

Duets:
September 2002—*Once Upon a Tiara/Henry Ever After* (#83)
October 2002—*Natalia's Story/Andrea's Story* (#85)

 Celebrate a year of royalty with Harlequin Books!

Available at your favorite retail outlet.

HARLEQUIN®
Makes any time special®

Visit us at www.eHarlequin.com

HSROY02

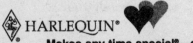

HARLEQUIN®

AMERICAN *Romance*®

invites you to meet the citizens
of Harmony, Arizona,
with a brand-new miniseries by

Sharon Swan

WELCOME
to Harmony

A little town with lots of surprises!

Don't miss any of these heartwarming tales:

HOME-GROWN HUSBAND
June 2002

HUSBANDS, HUSBANDS…EVERYWHERE!
September 2002

And look for more titles in 2003!

*Available wherever
Harlequin books are sold.*

HARLEQUIN®
Makes any time special ®

Visit us at www.eHarlequin.com

HARWTH